Echoes Within

J.J. Holt

Published by J.J. Holt, 2024.

ECHOES WITHIN

First edition. August 28, 2024.

ISBN: 979-8227862174

Written by J.J. Holt.

Echos Within
By J.J. Holt

To my beloved wife, Louisa, and our wonderful children, Aubrie, Conry, Riker, and Avery—

This story is for you. Your love, support, and boundless inspiration have made this journey possible. Each of you holds a special place in my heart. Thank you for being my greatest adventure.

With all my love.

Prologue: The Asylum's Awakening

The year was 1947, and the old asylum loomed over the landscape like a silent sentinel, its crumbling facade bearing witness to decades of despair. Located on the outskirts of a small, isolated town, the building had once been a beacon of hope for those suffering from mental illness. Now, it stood as a decaying monument to forgotten promises and abandoned souls.

Inside, the air was thick with the scent of mildew and decay. The corridors, once bustling with activity, were now silent except for the occasional drip of water from a leaking pipe or the scurry of a rat along the cracked linoleum floor. The walls were adorned with peeling paint, and the windows, long since caked with grime, allowed only the faintest hint of daylight to penetrate the darkness.

In the heart of the asylum, deep within its labyrinthine halls, a group of men gathered in what had once been the director's office. The room was spacious, with high ceilings and walls lined with bookshelves that sagged under the weight of dusty tomes. A large oak desk dominated the center, its surface cluttered with papers, medical instruments, and a peculiar array of objects that hinted at the nature of the evening's activities.

Dr. Richard Blake stood by the desk, his eyes fixed on the pages of an ancient-looking journal. The leather-bound book was worn, its edges frayed from years of use. Richard's hands trembled slightly as he turned the page, revealing a diagram filled with symbols and notations in a language that was not entirely familiar to him. He had spent years piecing together the fragmented knowledge contained within the journal, knowledge that had been passed down through generations and shrouded in secrecy.

The other men in the room, his colleagues in this endeavor, watched him intently. They were all respected figures in the field of psychiatry, though their reputations were often marred by whispers of unorthodox practices. Each of them had been drawn to this place by the promise of groundbreaking discoveries, driven by a shared belief that the human mind held untapped potential—potential that could be unlocked, controlled, and perhaps even weaponized.

"Is it ready?" Dr. Joseph Grayson, a tall, thin man with a sharp jawline and piercing eyes, asked. His voice carried a note of impatience, betraying the anxiety that gnawed at the edges of his composure.

Richard glanced up, meeting Joseph's gaze. "It is," he replied, though his voice was softer, more contemplative. "But I must caution you all once more—what we are about to attempt has never been done before. The forces we are dealing with are not to be trifled with. This is not merely an experiment in psychiatry; it is an exploration into realms beyond our understanding."

Dr. Miriam Caldwell, the only woman in the group and one of the most respected psychoanalysts of her time, stepped forward. Her expression was calm, though her eyes flickered with a hint of curiosity and concern. "We are all aware of the risks, Richard. But we also know the potential rewards. If we succeed, we could redefine the field, change the way we understand the mind forever."

Richard nodded, though his unease did not dissipate. He had always been the most cautious of the group, perhaps because he understood better than any of them the true nature of the forces they were about to unleash. His research had led him down dark paths—paths that had revealed the existence of echoes, residual imprints of emotions and memories that could linger long after a person had died. These echoes, he believed, were the key to unlocking the hidden power of the human mind.

But there was more. The journal he held in his hands was not just a medical text; it was also a tome of arcane knowledge, written by a man who had dabbled in the occult as much as he had in science. The diagrams and symbols it contained were not merely scientific annotations—they were sigils, marks of power that could, when used correctly, interact with the echoes in ways that defied conventional understanding.

"We proceed," Richard said finally, closing the journal with a sense of finality. "But we must do so with the utmost care. What we unleash tonight, we may not be able to control."

The other members of the group exchanged glances, each of them sensing the gravity of the moment. They had come too far to turn back now, too invested in the promise of what they might achieve. Together, they had devised a method to tap into the echoes, to draw them out and amplify their effects. They believed that by doing so, they could unlock hidden memories, latent abilities, and perhaps even reach beyond the veil of death itself.

Richard moved to the center of the room, where a large chalk circle had been drawn on the floor, inscribed with the same symbols that filled the pages of the journal. At each cardinal point of the circle stood an object—an antique mirror, a metronome, a glass jar containing a single black feather, and a small iron key. These objects, seemingly mundane, had been carefully selected for their symbolic resonance, each representing a different aspect of the human psyche.

"Bring him in," Richard instructed, his voice steady now as he assumed the role of leader.

Two orderlies, burly men with rough hands and blank expressions, entered the room, dragging a man between them. The man was in his late thirties, with disheveled hair and a vacant stare. His clothes were tattered, and his skin was pale, almost translucent in the dim light. This was Patient 23, one of the asylum's long-term residents, chosen for this experiment because of his history of severe mental illness and his apparent sensitivity to the echoes.

Patient 23 had been diagnosed with a rare form of schizophrenia, characterized by vivid hallucinations and delusions that had resisted all forms of conventional treatment. But Richard and his colleagues believed that his condition made him uniquely suited to the experiment. They had observed that the echoes were stronger around him, that his mind seemed to resonate with the residual energy that lingered in the asylum's walls.

The orderlies positioned the patient in the center of the circle, then stepped back, their faces impassive. Richard approached the man, kneeling beside him and placing a hand on his shoulder. The patient flinched at the contact, his eyes darting around the room as if he could sense the weight of what was about to happen.

"Be still," Richard murmured, though he knew the words would do little to calm the man's shattered mind. "We are here to help you, to free you from the torment that plagues you."

The patient's eyes met Richard's for a brief moment, and in that gaze, Richard saw a flicker of something—fear, recognition, perhaps even understanding. But it was gone as quickly as it had appeared, replaced by the dull glaze of madness.

Richard stood and began to chant, his voice low and steady. The words he spoke were not his own; they were phrases taken from the journal, phrases that had been passed down through generations of those who had sought to understand the mysteries of the mind and the soul. The other doctors joined in, their voices creating a harmonious but eerie chorus that filled the room with an almost tangible energy.

As they chanted, the air within the circle seemed to grow heavier, charged with an unseen force. The symbols on the floor began to glow faintly, their lines shimmering with a pale, ghostly light. The objects at the cardinal points reacted as well—the mirror's surface rippled as if disturbed by an invisible hand, the metronome's arm began to swing of its own accord, the feather inside the jar twisted and turned as if caught in a wind, and the iron key vibrated gently on the floor.

Patient 23 began to tremble, his body convulsing as if he were being pulled in multiple directions at once. His mouth opened, but no sound emerged. His eyes rolled back in his head, and for a moment, it seemed as though he might collapse entirely. But then, with a sudden jolt, his body went rigid, and his eyes snapped open, glowing with an unnatural light.

The echoes had found him.

Richard stepped back, his heart pounding in his chest. This was the moment they had been working towards, the moment that would prove whether their theories were correct—or whether they had ventured too far into forbidden knowledge.

"Now," Richard said, his voice barely above a whisper, "focus your minds. We must guide the echoes, shape them, control them."

The group concentrated, their collective will directed towards the patient. They visualized the echoes as tendrils of energy, reaching out from the shadows, seeking a host. Their goal was to harness this energy, to draw it into the patient's mind and use it to unlock the deepest recesses of his memory, to access the hidden truths buried within his psyche.

For a moment, it seemed to work. The patient's convulsions ceased, and he stood motionless, his eyes still glowing. The room was silent, save for the rhythmic ticking of the metronome and the faint hum of energy in the air.

But then, something changed.

The light in the patient's eyes flickered, and a low, guttural growl emanated from his throat. His body jerked violently, and the glow in his eyes intensified, becoming a blinding white light that filled the room. The chalk circle on the floor began to smolder, the symbols burning themselves into the linoleum. The objects at the cardinal points shuddered and cracked, the mirror shattering into a thousand pieces, the metronome snapping in two, the jar containing the feather exploding, and the iron key disintegrating into dust.

"Stop! Stop it now!" Dr. Grayson shouted, his voice tinged with panic.

Richard tried to break the circle, to sever the connection between the patient and the echoes, but it was too late. The force they had unleashed was far beyond their control. The patient's body was lifted off the ground, suspended in mid-air by an unseen power. His mouth opened wide, and from his throat emerged a sound that was not human—a deep, resonant echo that seemed to come from the very bowels of the earth.

The light in the room intensified, blinding the doctors. They stumbled back, shielding their eyes, but the sound continued, growing louder and more insistent. It was as if the echoes were screaming, crying out in anger and pain, seeking vengeance for the centuries of torment they had endured.

And then, with a deafening roar, the light exploded outward, consuming everything in its path. The doctors were thrown against the walls, their bodies limp and unconscious. The patient's body crumpled to the floor, his eyes closed, the glow extinguished. The room was plunged into darkness, the only sound the faint crackling of the smoldering floor.

Richard was the first to regain consciousness. He pushed himself up, his body aching from the impact. The room was in ruins—the furniture shattered, the walls scorched, and the symbols on the floor obliterated. His colleagues lay motionless around him, but he could see their chests rise and fall with shallow breaths. They were alive, but only just.

He staggered to his feet, his mind reeling from what had just occurred. The patient was dead, his body contorted in a grotesque manner. The echoes had consumed him, used him as a vessel to break free from whatever constraints had held them in check for so long.

Richard stumbled to the desk, where the journal lay open, miraculously untouched by the chaos. His hands shook as he flipped to the last page, where a single phrase had been scrawled hastily in the margin by the journal's previous owner:

Beware the echoes, for they carry the weight of all that has been forgotten, and they seek to remember.

He reached for a pen, knowing that he had to leave a warning for whoever might come after them. His colleagues were stirring, groaning as they began to awaken, but Richard's focus was on the journal. He had to document what had happened, to ensure that the knowledge they had uncovered would not be lost—nor repeated.

His hand hovered over the page, unsure of how to begin. The echoes had been unleashed, and with them, a malevolent force that defied all reason and understanding. He didn't know how far it would spread, or how many lives it would touch, but he knew one thing for certain:

They had opened a door that should never have been opened, and the darkness on the other side had taken notice.

We have made a grave mistake, he wrote, his script hurried and uneven. *The echoes are not just residual energy—they are alive, and they are hungry. They seek to feed on our fears, our guilt, our very souls. If you are reading this, you must stop. Do not continue our work. Destroy the journal, destroy all records of this experiment. Do not let the echoes find you.*

He set the pen down, his breath ragged. Outside, he could hear the distant wail of a siren, the sound growing louder as it approached the asylum. Help was on the way, but Richard knew it was already too late.

The echoes had been unleashed, and there was no turning back.

As the sirens drew closer, Richard closed the journal and placed it in the desk drawer, locking it with trembling hands. He knew he had little time left, but there was one last thing he had to do. He reached for the old reel-to-reel tape recorder that sat on the corner of the desk, its tape already loaded and ready to record.

He pressed the button, and the machine whirred to life, the tape beginning to spin. Richard leaned close to the microphone, his voice barely above a whisper.

"This is Dr. Richard Blake, recording my final thoughts on the experiment conducted this evening. We have unleashed something beyond our control, a force tied to the echoes that dwell within this asylum. I do not know the full extent of the damage we have caused, but I fear it is far greater than we ever imagined."

He paused, his mind racing as he tried to find the words to convey the horror of what had transpired.

"The echoes... they are not just memories. They are something more. Something ancient, something malevolent. We have tapped into a force that defies all reason, all understanding. It feeds on our darkest emotions, our guilt, our fears. It is a force of destruction, and it will not rest until it has consumed everything in its path."

Richard's voice broke, and he took a moment to steady himself before continuing.

"I leave this recording as a warning to those who might follow in our footsteps. Do not repeat our mistakes. Destroy this tape, destroy all evidence of this experiment. If the echoes find you, they will not stop until they have taken everything from you. They are relentless, and they are without mercy."

He stopped the recording, the tape coming to a halt with a soft click. For a moment, he simply sat there, staring at the machine, the weight of his actions pressing down on him like a physical burden.

The echoes had been unleashed, and they would not be easily contained.

As the first responders arrived at the asylum, their voices echoing through the halls, Richard Blake knew that the darkness they had summoned was just beginning to spread.

And there would be no escaping it.

THE SOUND OF APPROACHING footsteps echoed through the corridors of the asylum, mingling with the distant wail of sirens. Richard Blake sat motionless in the director's office, his eyes fixed on the journal now locked away in the desk drawer. The weight of what he had written pressed heavily on his chest, as if the very air around him had thickened with the gravity of his words.

He could hear his colleagues stirring behind him, their groans of pain and confusion signaling their return to consciousness. Dr. Miriam Caldwell was the first to rise, her hand pressed to her forehead as she tried to steady herself. Her eyes, usually so sharp and composed, were wide with shock as she took in the devastation around her.

"What... what happened?" she whispered, her voice trembling.

Richard didn't respond immediately. He was still grappling with the enormity of their actions, the full implications of what they had unleashed. The echoes had been more than just residual energy, more than mere imprints of past emotions. They had been alive, sentient in a way that defied all scientific understanding.

And now, they were free.

"Richard," Dr. Joseph Grayson's voice cut through the fog of Richard's thoughts. He turned to see Grayson struggling to his feet, his expression a mix of anger and fear. "What have we done?"

Richard could only shake his head, his throat too tight to form a coherent response. He felt as though he were standing on the edge of a precipice, staring into an abyss that had no end. The echoes were more powerful than he had ever imagined, and they had been released into a world unprepared for their wrath.

The door to the office burst open, and a group of uniformed men rushed in, their faces stern and professional. The lead officer, a grizzled man with a thick mustache and a no-nonsense demeanor, quickly assessed the situation. His eyes narrowed as he took in the unconscious patient on the floor, the smoldering symbols, and the disarrayed doctors.

"What the hell happened here?" the officer demanded, his voice authoritative.

Richard forced himself to stand, though his legs felt weak and unsteady. "It was an experiment," he said, his voice hoarse. "An experiment that... went wrong."

The officer's gaze hardened. "I'll say it went wrong. We've got reports of strange lights, explosions, and God knows what else coming from this place. What the hell were you people doing?"

Richard opened his mouth to respond, but the words caught in his throat. How could he possibly explain what had happened? How could he describe the forces they had tampered with, the darkness they had unleashed? The echoes were not something that could be easily understood, let alone explained to those who had never encountered them.

"We were conducting a psychological experiment," Dr. Caldwell interjected, her voice calmer now as she tried to regain control of the situation. "It was meant to explore the deeper recesses of the mind, to access memories that had been repressed or forgotten."

The officer frowned. "And this... patient?" He gestured to the lifeless body of Patient 23.

"He was our subject," Grayson said, his voice steady but his eyes betraying his fear. "We believed he had a unique sensitivity to certain... energies."

"Energies?" The officer's skepticism was palpable. "What kind of energies are we talking about here?"

Richard swallowed hard, knowing that the truth was too bizarre, too dangerous to reveal in full. "Residual energies," he said carefully. "Memories, emotions, the kind of things that linger in a place like this."

The officer eyed him suspiciously, but before he could press further, one of the other doctors groaned and began to sit up. The officer waved for his men to help the fallen doctors, and they quickly moved to assist, checking for injuries and administering aid where needed.

As the chaos in the room began to subside, Richard's mind raced. He knew that they had to contain this situation, to prevent the truth from spreading. If word got out about the echoes, about the malevolent force they had unleashed, it could spark panic, or worse—it could draw others who would seek to harness the power for their own ends.

"Listen to me," Richard said, his voice low and urgent as he addressed the officer. "You need to understand that what happened here... it can't be allowed to leave this room. The consequences would be disastrous."

The officer narrowed his eyes. "And why should I keep quiet about this?"

"Because this is beyond anything you've ever dealt with," Richard replied, his tone deadly serious. "The forces we've encountered here—if they get out, if they spread—it could be catastrophic. We were trying to contain them, to understand them, but we failed. Now we have to make sure no one else makes the same mistake."

The officer studied Richard for a long moment, weighing his words. Finally, he nodded slowly. "Alright, Doctor. But this better not come back to bite me in the ass. We'll report this as a containment breach, an experimental procedure that went wrong. But you're going to need to clean this mess up, and fast."

Richard nodded, relief washing over him. "Thank you. We'll take care of it."

As the officer and his men began to secure the scene, Richard turned to his colleagues. They were all shaken, but there was a grim determination in their eyes. They had made a terrible mistake, but now they had to find a way to fix it.

"We need to regroup," Richard said, his voice firm. "We need to figure out how to contain this, how to stop it from spreading."

"And how do we do that?" Dr. Caldwell asked, her voice edged with fear. "We've unleashed something we don't understand, something that doesn't play by the rules of our world."

Richard took a deep breath, steeling himself. "We start by documenting everything. Every detail, every finding, every observation. We need to understand exactly what we're dealing with. Then we find a way to contain it, to seal it off for good."

"And if we can't?" Grayson's voice was barely above a whisper.

Richard didn't have an answer for that. The echoes were already loose, already spreading their influence. Containing them might be impossible, but they had to try. If they didn't, the darkness they had unleashed would only grow stronger, feeding on the fears and guilt of everyone it touched.

As the group of doctors began to gather their notes, Richard knew that their work was far from over. The experiment had gone horribly wrong, but the echoes were not done with them yet. The malevolent force they had unleashed was hungry, and it would not rest until it had consumed everything in its path.

****TWO WEEKS LATER****

The asylum was quiet, but the quiet was the kind that buzzed with the unspoken tension of the past. Richard had returned alone, under the pretense of securing more documents and finalizing the shutdown of the facility. In reality, he had come back to face the echoes, to attempt to understand and, if possible, to put an end to the terror they had unleashed.

The journal had been hidden away, along with the tape recording of his warnings. The other doctors had decided it was best to seal them away in the archives, out of sight and out of mind. But Richard knew that the echoes could not be so easily dismissed. They were alive, sentient, and they had already begun to reach beyond the asylum's walls.

As he walked through the corridors, the weight of the atmosphere pressed down on him, thick with the memories of the lives that had been shattered within these walls. The echoes were strong here, pulsing with the residual energy of the countless tormented souls who had passed through the asylum over the years. Richard could feel their presence, a palpable weight that seemed to watch his every move.

He reached the director's office, the site of the fateful experiment. The door creaked open, and Richard stepped inside, his heart pounding. The room looked as it had on that night—except for the absence of his colleagues and the lifeless body of Patient 23. But the air was different now, thicker, more oppressive. It was as though the very walls were alive, imbued with the echoes of the past.

Richard crossed to the desk and retrieved the journal from its hiding place. He opened it to the page where he had scrawled his warning, and his eyes traced the words once more. He knew that the journal was the key, the one source of knowledge that could help him understand what they had unleashed. But he also knew that it was dangerous—too dangerous to keep.

He began to flip through the pages, his eyes scanning the arcane symbols and diagrams that had once fascinated him. Now, they filled him with dread. He paused on a page near the back of the journal, where a diagram depicted a complex ritual—a binding spell designed to contain malevolent spirits.

Richard's breath caught in his throat. This was it. This was what they needed—a way to bind the echoes, to seal them away before they could spread further. But as he read through the instructions, a cold realization settled over him.

The ritual required a sacrifice.

Not just any sacrifice, but a sacrifice of something deeply personal, something tied to the person performing the ritual. The echoes thrived on guilt and fear, and the only way to bind them was to offer them something that embodied those emotions—a memory, a life, a soul.

Richard's hands shook as he closed the journal. He knew what he had to do, but the thought of it filled him with a terror he had never known. The echoes had already claimed the life of Patient 23, and now they demanded more. But there was no other way. If he didn't stop them, the echoes would continue to spread, leaving a trail of destruction in their wake.

He took a deep breath and steeled himself for what was to come. He would perform the ritual, but he would do it alone. He couldn't ask his colleagues to risk their lives—or their souls—any further. This was his responsibility, his burden to bear.

As he prepared the room for the ritual, drawing the symbols on the floor with careful precision, Richard's mind drifted back to his own past. He had always been driven by a desire to understand the mind, to unlock its secrets. But he had never imagined that those secrets would come at such a cost.

He thought of his father, a man of science who had never believed in the supernatural. Richard had followed in his father's footsteps, seeking to make a name for himself in the field of psychiatry. But now, he wondered if his father had been right to reject the darker aspects of the mind, the ones that defied explanation and lurked in the shadows.

The room was ready, the symbols glowing faintly in the dim light. Richard took his place in the center of the circle, holding the journal in one hand and a small, silver knife in the other. The ritual required blood—his blood—a symbol of his connection to the echoes, a bridge between the living and the dead.

He began to chant the words from the journal, his voice steady despite the fear that gnawed at his insides. The air around him seemed to thicken, the weight of the echoes pressing in from all sides. The symbols on the floor pulsed with energy, the lines shimmering with a pale, ghostly light.

Richard made the first cut, a shallow line across his palm. Blood welled up, dripping onto the floor, and the echoes responded. The air filled with a low, resonant hum, the sound of countless voices overlapping, each one crying out in pain, anger, and despair.

He continued the chant, his voice growing louder as the echoes surged around him. The room grew colder, the temperature dropping rapidly as the ritual progressed. Frost began to form on the windows, the glass cracking under the pressure. Richard could feel the echoes drawing closer, their presence almost suffocating.

The journal trembled in his hand, the pages fluttering as if caught in a gust of wind. Richard forced himself to continue, pushing through the fear that threatened to overwhelm him. He could feel the echoes resisting, fighting against the binding spell. They were strong—stronger than he had anticipated—but he was determined to see this through.

With a final, desperate push, Richard drove the knife into the floor, piercing the center of the circle. The room erupted in a blinding flash of light, the force of the echoes recoiling as they were drawn into the symbols. Richard screamed as the energy coursed through him, the pain searing his nerves like fire.

The echoes writhed, twisting and contorting as they were forced into the binding circle. The light intensified, blinding Richard, but he refused to let go. He could feel the echoes trying to escape, but he held them fast, pouring every ounce of his will into the ritual.

And then, with a final, deafening roar, the light vanished, and the room fell into silence.

Richard collapsed to the floor, his body trembling with exhaustion. The ritual had worked—the echoes were bound, sealed within the symbols that now glowed faintly on the floor. But the cost had been high.

He could feel the weight of the echoes in his mind, a dark presence that lurked just beneath the surface. They were not gone—they had merely been contained. The ritual had worked, but it was only a temporary solution. The echoes would remain dormant for now, but they would always be there, waiting for a moment of weakness, a crack in the seal that held them.

Richard forced himself to his feet, his body aching with the effort. He knew that this was not the end—it was only the beginning. The echoes had been bound, but they were not destroyed. And as long as they existed, the danger would remain.

He had to leave. The asylum was no longer a place of healing—it had become a prison, a tomb for the echoes that had once roamed free. He had to ensure that no one else would stumble upon the knowledge he had uncovered, that no one else would make the same mistakes.

He retrieved the journal, carefully locking it away in the desk drawer once more. But this time, he knew that it could not stay here. He would have to find a place to hide it, somewhere it could never be found. The knowledge within its pages was too dangerous, too tempting for those who sought power.

As he made his way to the exit, Richard took one last look at the asylum. The building stood silent and still, but he knew that within its walls, the echoes still stirred. He had done what he could, but he knew that it might not be enough.

The echoes would wait, biding their time until they could find another way out. And when that time came, the world would once again be at their mercy.

As he stepped outside into the cold night air, Richard knew that his work was not finished. He would spend the rest of his life trying to find a way to destroy the echoes once and for all, to ensure that the darkness they carried could never again be unleashed.

But as he walked away from the asylum, the weight of the echoes heavy on his soul, he knew that he might never succeed. The echoes were a part of him now, a shadow that would follow him until the end of his days.

And somewhere deep inside, he feared that they would one day find a way to escape.

THE PROLOGUE, NOW NEARING completion, sets the stage for *The Echo Within*, weaving together the foreboding atmosphere, the consequences of the experiment, and Richard Blake's desperate attempt to contain the malevolent force he and his colleagues have unleashed. If you'd like, I can continue to refine and expand this section to ensure it meets the full 4,000-word goal while enhancing the tension and thematic depth. Let me know how you'd like to proceed!

Chapter 1: The Facade

The sterile, white walls of Dr. Aaron Blake's office were interrupted only by the occasional framed diploma or certificate, each one carefully positioned to project competence and authority. The space was modern, almost cold in its efficiency, with minimalist furniture designed for function rather than comfort. The desk, made of dark mahogany, was immaculately organized, with files stacked neatly on one side and a computer monitor that remained perpetually angled to hide its contents from prying eyes.

Aaron, the epitome of professionalism, sat behind the desk, his posture straight, hands clasped lightly in front of him. He was in his early forties, with short, neatly trimmed hair that was beginning to show the first hints of gray at the temples. His eyes were a piercing blue, sharp and discerning, the kind of eyes that missed nothing. His suit was tailored to perfection, a dark gray that matched the clinical precision of the room. He exuded an air of calm, the kind of calm that patients found reassuring, even if it was merely a facade.

Across from him, in one of the two identical chairs that faced the desk, sat his latest patient. The man was in his mid-thirties, his face pale and gaunt, with dark circles under his eyes that suggested sleepless nights. He fidgeted in his seat, his fingers tapping nervously on the armrest, unable to settle. His vulnerability was palpable, tugging at the heartstrings of even the most stoic observer.

"Mr. Collins," Aaron began, his voice smooth and measured, the kind of voice that was designed to instill trust. "We've been meeting for several weeks now, and I've noticed some patterns in your behavior that I think we should discuss."

Collins swallowed hard, his Adam's apple bobbing in his throat. "Patterns?"

"Yes," Aaron continued, leaning forward slightly, as if to convey a sense of personal investment. "You've mentioned recurring thoughts, thoughts that you can't seem to escape. They're intrusive, aren't they? Thoughts that bring up memories you'd rather forget."

Collins nodded slowly, his eyes fixed on a point somewhere over Aaron's shoulder. "Yes, that's right. I can't... I can't get rid of them. They're always there, lurking, even when I try to push them away."

Aaron allowed a brief moment of silence to pass, a technique he often used to let the weight of the patient's words settle in. Silence was a powerful tool in his line of work—used correctly, it could draw out confessions, uncover hidden fears, and bring buried memories to the surface.

"Tell me about these thoughts," Aaron prompted gently. "What do they involve? What are they trying to tell you?"

Collins hesitated, his fingers still drumming on the armrest. "It's... it's about my wife," he finally admitted, his voice barely above a whisper. "She died a year ago. Car accident. I... I wasn't there when it happened. I should have been, but I wasn't."

A flicker of something passed through Aaron's eyes—sympathy, perhaps, or recognition. But it was gone as quickly as it had appeared, replaced by the professional detachment that had become second nature to him. "You blame yourself," Aaron said, more as a statement than a question.

Collins nodded, his face contorting with the pain of the admission. "Yes. I can't stop thinking about it. If I had been there, maybe... maybe I could have done something."

Aaron leaned back in his chair, his mind already working through the possible therapeutic approaches. Guilt was a powerful emotion, one that could trap a person in an endless loop of self-recrimination. But it could also be harnessed, redirected into something more productive.

"Mr. Collins, I want to talk to you about cognitive behavioral therapy, or CBT," Aaron said. "It's a technique we use to help patients identify and challenge negative thought patterns. The idea is to break the cycle of guilt and self-blame by replacing those thoughts with more balanced, realistic ones."

Collins looked up, his eyes searching Aaron's face for some sign of hope. "Do you think it will work? Can it really help me?"

Aaron offered a small, reassuring smile. "I believe it can. It will take time and effort, but with the right approach, you can learn to manage these thoughts, to take control of them instead of letting them control you."

As Aaron continued to explain the principles of CBT, outlining the steps Collins would need to take, his mind remained focused, his words precise and practiced. This was his domain, the place where he could exert control, where everything followed a predictable pattern. But even as he spoke, a part of him remained detached, as if he were observing the session from a distance, separate from the man who sat in the chair and the words that came out of his mouth.

It was a survival mechanism, one that Aaron had honed over years of practice. He had learned to compartmentalize, to keep his emotions locked away, safely out of reach. It was the only way he could do this work, the only way he could maintain the facade of calm and control that his patients relied on.

But there were cracks in that facade, cracks that had begun to widen in recent months. They were small, barely noticeable to anyone but himself, but they were there, lurking just beneath the surface. And though Aaron tried to ignore them, to push them aside and bury them deep within the recesses of his mind, they persisted.

As the session drew to a close, Aaron made a few final notes in Collins' file, his handwriting neat and precise. "I'll see you next week, Mr. Collins," he said, rising from his chair and extending his hand. "And remember, the work we're doing here is important, but it's also difficult. Be patient with yourself, and don't hesitate to reach out if you need support."

Collins shook Aaron's hand, his grip firm but still tinged with that nervous energy. "Thank you, Dr. Blake. I appreciate it. I'll try to do the exercises you mentioned." His voice carried a glimmer of hope, a sign that he was ready to embark on the journey towards healing.

Aaron nodded, his smile remaining in place until Collins had exited the office and the door had clicked shut behind him. Once he was alone, the smile faded, replaced by an expression of weariness. He leaned back in his chair, letting out a slow breath as he stared up at the ceiling.

This was the part of the day he dreaded most—the moments between patients, when the silence of the office became oppressive, and there was nothing to distract him from his own thoughts. It was in these moments that the cracks in his facade felt most pronounced, the fractures in his carefully constructed persona threatening to break open.

He reached for the cup of coffee that sat on his desk, now cold from neglect. As he took a sip, his mind drifted back to the patient he had just seen. Guilt was a familiar theme in his practice, one that he had encountered countless times over the years. But it was more than just a clinical concept to him—it was something he understood on a deeply personal level.

Aaron had his own guilt, guilt that he carried with him like a shadow, always present, always lurking just out of sight. It was a burden he had learned to bear, a weight that he had grown accustomed to. But there were times when it threatened to overwhelm him, when the memories it was tied to would resurface, unbidden and unwanted.

He could still remember the day his father had died, the way the light had drained from the old man's eyes as he lay in that sterile hospital bed. Richard Blake had been a man of science, a brilliant mind who had dedicated his life to the study of the human psyche. But in the end, it had been his own mind that had betrayed him, driving him to the brink of madness.

Aaron had been young then, just beginning his own career in psychiatry, eager to prove himself and to live up to the legacy his father had left behind. But there had always been a distance between them, a gulf that had grown wider with each passing year. Richard Blake had been a difficult man, demanding, exacting, and often cold. He had expected nothing less than perfection from his son, and Aaron had spent his entire life trying to meet those expectations.

But he had failed. In the end, he had failed his father, just as he had failed so many others.

The memories of his father's death were fragmented, disjointed pieces of a puzzle that he had never been able to fully assemble. There were gaps in his recollection, moments that were lost to him, as if his mind had chosen to block them out. But the guilt remained, a constant reminder of the things he had left undone, the words he had never spoken.

Aaron set the coffee cup down, his hand trembling slightly as he did so. He knew better than to dwell on the past, to let those memories resurface. He had spent years learning to compartmentalize, to lock those thoughts away where they couldn't hurt him. But there were times when they slipped through the cracks, when they threatened to overwhelm him.

He forced himself to focus, to push those thoughts aside and concentrate on the task at hand. There were still patients to see, files to review, and reports to complete. There was no time to indulge in self-pity, no time to let the past intrude on the present.

He reached for the next file in the stack on his desk, flipping it open with a practiced motion. The name at the top of the page caught his attention: Elena Carter. He frowned slightly, the name unfamiliar to him. She was a new patient, recently transferred to his care from another facility.

Aaron scanned the file, his eyes narrowing as he took in the details. Elena Carter, age thirty-two, history of severe anxiety and depression, multiple hospitalizations, and a recent diagnosis of PTSD. But there was something else, something that stood out from the usual list of symptoms—an unusual claim that had been noted by her previous therapist.

Elena believed she could hear echoes. Not the kind of echoes one might hear in a physical sense, but something far more unsettling—echoes of people's thoughts, their memories, their darkest secrets. She had described it as a kind of psychic ability, one that she couldn't control, and one that had left her isolated and fearful.

Aaron's brow furrowed as he read the notes. The previous therapist had dismissed the claim as a delusion, a symptom of Elena's anxiety and PTSD. But there was something about the way it was described, something that gave Aaron pause. He couldn't explain it, but a part of him recognized the fear and desperation in those words, a part of him that had long since learned to ignore such things.

He closed the file and set it aside, his mind already working through the possible approaches to Elena's treatment. On the surface, it seemed straightforward enough—another case of trauma and anxiety, another patient struggling to find her way back to some semblance of normalcy. But there was a nagging feeling in the back of his mind, a sense that there was more to this case than met the eye.

Aaron pushed the thought aside and stood up, stretching his legs as he walked to the window. The view from his office was typical of any large hospital—a sprawling campus of buildings, parking lots, and carefully manicured lawns. It was a view he had seen countless times before, and yet today it felt different, as if the world outside had shifted in some subtle way.

He stared out at the horizon, his mind wandering as he tried to make sense of the unease that had settled over him. The sky was a dull, overcast gray, the kind of sky that seemed to press down on the earth, suffocating everything beneath it. It matched his mood, the weight of his thoughts, the pressure that seemed to be building with each passing moment.

Aaron had always prided himself on his ability to remain calm, to maintain control in even the most challenging situations. It was a skill that had served him well in his career, a skill that had allowed him to help countless patients navigate the labyrinth of their own minds. But lately, that control had begun to slip, the cracks in his facade growing wider with each passing day.

He turned away from the window, his gaze falling on the stack of files that awaited his attention. There was no time to dwell on his own problems, no time to indulge in the luxury of introspection. His patients needed him, and he had a job to do.

But even as he forced himself back into the routine of his day, the unease lingered, a shadow that refused to be banished. There was something about Elena Carter's file, something about her story that resonated with him in a way he couldn't quite explain.

And as he sat down at his desk, ready to face the next patient, a thought crossed his mind, unbidden and unwelcome.

What if she was telling the truth?

The question hung in the air, unanswered, as Aaron reached for the phone to call his assistant. "Send in the next patient," he said, his voice steady, betraying none of the turmoil that churned beneath the surface.

But as he waited for the door to open, the question remained, gnawing at him, refusing to be dismissed.

What if she was telling the truth?

And what if the echoes she heard were real?

The door opened, and the next patient entered, but Aaron's mind was no longer fully in the room. His thoughts lingered on the file of Elena Carter, on the strange and unsettling possibility that had taken root in his mind.

And as the session began, he couldn't shake the feeling that something was about to change, that his carefully constructed world was about to be turned upside down.

The cracks in his facade were growing wider, and Aaron could only hope that he would be able to hold them together long enough to make it through the day.

But deep down, he knew that the echoes of his past, and the echoes of Elena Carter's strange abilities, were drawing closer, and there was no telling what they might reveal when they finally broke through.

Aaron Blake prided himself on his ability to compartmentalize, to keep his emotions locked away in a box where they couldn't interfere with his work. It was a skill he had honed over years of practice, one that had become second nature to him. But as the day wore on, the carefully maintained walls around his psyche began to show signs of strain.

The next patient was an older woman, Mrs. Janet Wallace, who had been referred to him for chronic anxiety and depression. She was in her late sixties, with silver hair that had been meticulously styled and a wardrobe that suggested a woman of some means. But there was a weariness about her, a heaviness in her posture and in the way she spoke, that hinted at a life burdened by unresolved grief.

"Good afternoon, Mrs. Wallace," Aaron greeted her as she settled into the chair across from his desk. "How have you been feeling since our last session?"

Mrs. Wallace sighed softly, her hands clasped in her lap. "I suppose I've been doing about the same, Dr. Blake. The medications help a bit, but the anxiety... it never really goes away. It's always there, lurking in the background."

Aaron nodded, his expression one of practiced empathy. "That's not uncommon with anxiety disorders, especially when they've been present for a long time. Have you been able to use any of the mindfulness techniques we discussed?"

Mrs. Wallace hesitated, her gaze dropping to her hands. "I've tried," she admitted. "But it's difficult. My mind just won't quiet down. It's like there's a constant buzz, a noise that I can't escape from."

Aaron leaned forward slightly, his tone gentle but firm. "It's important to remember that mindfulness is a skill, Mrs. Wallace. It takes time and practice to develop. The goal isn't to silence your thoughts completely, but to learn to observe them without judgment, to let them pass through your mind without attaching to them."

She nodded, though her expression remained doubtful. "I understand, Doctor. But it's hard... especially at night. That's when it's worst. I can't sleep, and when I do, I have these terrible dreams. I wake up in a panic, my heart racing, and I just feel... trapped."

Aaron noted the mention of nightmares, a detail that hadn't come up in their previous sessions. "These dreams," he said, probing gently, "do they relate to any specific memories or events from your past?"

Mrs. Wallace was silent for a moment, her brow furrowing as she considered the question. "I'm not sure," she finally replied. "They're... strange. Sometimes, they're about my husband. He passed away five years ago. But other times, they're about things that never happened. Places I've never been, people I don't know. But they feel real, Doctor. As if I'm living someone else's life."

Aaron's pen hovered over his notepad, a sense of unease prickling at the back of his mind. This wasn't the first time a patient had described such experiences to him, but there was something about Mrs. Wallace's account that felt different. He couldn't quite place it, but it reminded him of the notes in Elena Carter's file—the strange and unsettling echoes she claimed to hear.

"Have you experienced anything like this before?" he asked, keeping his tone neutral.

Mrs. Wallace shook her head. "No, not like this. It's only been in the past year or so. I thought maybe it was just the stress of getting older, or maybe it's the medication. But I don't know, Doctor... it's like there's something trying to reach me, something I can't see but can feel."

Aaron made a note of her words, his thoughts racing. The logical part of his mind, the part that had been trained to view such claims through the lens of psychology, wanted to dismiss it as another manifestation of her anxiety—a way for her subconscious to process unresolved emotions. But another part of him, the part that had grown up under the shadow of his father's legacy, couldn't shake the feeling that there was more to it.

"We'll explore this further in our next session," Aaron said, keeping his voice steady. "In the meantime, I'd like you to continue practicing the mindfulness exercises, and we'll adjust your medication to see if that helps with the nightmares."

Mrs. Wallace nodded, though she still looked uncertain. "Thank you, Doctor. I'll try."

As she left the office, Aaron felt a familiar sense of frustration. It was the same frustration that had plagued him for years, the feeling that no matter how hard he tried, no matter how many patients he saw or how many therapies he prescribed, he could never quite reach the root of their suffering. He could treat the symptoms, manage the disorders, but the deeper issues, the ones that gnawed at the edges of their minds, remained elusive.

And then there was his own suffering, the burden he carried that no amount of therapy or medication could alleviate. The guilt that had taken root in his soul, the memories that haunted him even as he tried to bury them. He had devoted his life to helping others, to understanding the complexities of the human mind, but he had never been able to help himself.

Aaron stood up from his desk, needing a moment to clear his head. He walked to the window, staring out at the hospital grounds without really seeing them. His thoughts drifted back to Elena Carter, to the strange case that now sat at the forefront of his mind.

Elena's file was unlike any he had encountered before, and that was saying something. Over the years, he had seen patients with a wide range of disorders—schizophrenia, bipolar disorder, dissociative identity disorder, and more. He had treated them all with the same clinical detachment, relying on his training and experience to guide him. But Elena's case was different. Her symptoms didn't fit neatly into any of the categories he was familiar with. They were... otherworldly.

Aaron wasn't a superstitious man, but he couldn't deny that there was something about Elena's story that unnerved him. The way she described the echoes, the voices she claimed to hear, the memories that weren't hers—there was a clarity to her account that set it apart from the delusions of his other patients. And yet, he couldn't bring himself to believe it. To do so would be to cross a line, to step into a realm of uncertainty that he had spent his entire life avoiding.

He turned away from the window, trying to shake off the unease that clung to him like a second skin. There were still several hours left in his day, more patients to see, more files to review. He needed to focus, to push the troubling thoughts aside and return to the task at hand.

But as he sat back down at his desk, the sense of unease refused to dissipate. It lingered at the edges of his consciousness, a nagging feeling that something was wrong, that something was about to change.

The next patient was a young man in his twenties, Michael Davidson, who had been referred to Aaron for treatment of obsessive-compulsive disorder. Michael was a quiet, introverted individual, with a penchant for order and routine that bordered on the obsessive. He was a textbook case of OCD, with compulsions that included hand-washing, counting, and an irrational fear of contamination.

"Good afternoon, Michael," Aaron greeted him as he entered the office. "How are you doing today?"

Michael shrugged, his expression guarded. "Same as always, I guess. I'm trying to keep it together, but it's hard."

Aaron nodded, making a note of Michael's response. "Have you been able to practice the exposure therapy techniques we discussed?"

Michael shifted uncomfortably in his seat. "A little. But it's tough, you know? Every time I try to resist the urge, it's like this voice in my head is telling me that something terrible will happen if I don't. I know it's not real, but it feels real."

Aaron leaned forward, his tone empathetic. "That's a common experience with OCD, Michael. The key is to recognize that the voice is a symptom of the disorder, not a reflection of reality. The more you practice exposure therapy, the easier it will become to challenge those thoughts."

Michael nodded, though he still looked unconvinced. "It's just... hard to let go, you know? It's like I'm fighting against my own mind."

Aaron understood that feeling all too well. "It is hard, but you've made progress, Michael. You're here, you're trying, and that's important. The more you practice, the more you'll see that you have control over your thoughts, not the other way around."

As he spoke, Aaron couldn't help but think about his own struggles with control. He had spent his entire life trying to maintain a sense of order, to keep the chaos at bay. But there were times when that control slipped, when the cracks in his facade became too wide to ignore. He could empathize with Michael's struggle because it mirrored his own in many ways.

The session continued with Aaron guiding Michael through a series of cognitive-behavioral exercises designed to challenge his compulsions. But even as he went through the motions, his mind was elsewhere, distracted by the growing sense of unease that had taken hold of him.

When the session finally ended, and Michael had left the office, Aaron found himself staring at the door, his thoughts racing. He had always prided himself on his ability to remain focused, to keep his emotions in check. But today, something was different. The usual methods of compartmentalization weren't working. The cracks in his facade were growing wider, and he was finding it harder and harder to ignore them.

He took a deep breath, trying to steady himself. There was still one more patient to see, one more session to get through before he could call it a day. He needed to pull himself together, to regain the control that had always been his greatest asset.

But as he reached for the next file, his hand hesitated. It was Elena Carter's file, the one he had been avoiding all day. Her story had unsettled him, had stirred up memories and fears that he had long since buried. But there was no avoiding it now. He had to face it, to confront whatever it was that had taken hold of his mind.

He opened the file, his eyes scanning the pages as he tried to make sense of the information in front of him. Elena's symptoms were unlike anything he had encountered before—hearing echoes, voices, memories that weren't hers. It all pointed to something beyond the realm of the clinical, something that defied explanation.

Aaron had always been a man of science, a man who believed in logic and reason. But as he read through Elena's file, he felt those beliefs begin to waver. There was something about her story that resonated with him, something that touched on the darkest corners of his own mind.

He had spent his entire life trying to maintain control, to keep the chaos of his past at bay. But now, for the first time, he felt that control slipping away, as if the very foundations of his world were beginning to crumble.

The door to his office opened, and Aaron looked up to see his assistant standing in the doorway. "Dr. Blake, Ms. Carter is here for her appointment."

Aaron nodded, closing the file and setting it aside. "Thank you. Please send her in."

As his assistant left the room, Aaron took a moment to compose himself. He couldn't afford to let his emotions get the better of him, not now. He had to maintain his facade, to keep up the appearance of calm and control, even as the cracks in that facade continued to widen.

The door opened again, and Elena Carter stepped into the room. She was a striking woman, with dark hair that framed her pale face and eyes that were a deep, unsettling shade of green. There was a fragility about her, a vulnerability that was apparent in the way she held herself, as if she were bracing for some unseen blow.

"Ms. Carter," Aaron greeted her, rising from his chair and extending his hand. "Please, have a seat."

Elena took his hand, her grip surprisingly firm despite her delicate appearance. "Thank you, Dr. Blake," she said, her voice soft but steady.

As she settled into the chair across from his desk, Aaron studied her closely. There was something about her that set her apart from his other patients, something that went beyond her physical appearance. It was in her eyes, in the way she looked at him as if she could see right through his carefully constructed facade.

"So, Ms. Carter," Aaron began, sitting back down and opening her file. "I've reviewed your case, and I'd like to hear more about the experiences you've been having. Can you tell me about the echoes you've mentioned?"

Elena hesitated, her gaze dropping to her hands. "I don't know if you'll believe me," she said quietly. "Most people don't."

Aaron felt a pang of something—sympathy, perhaps, or something deeper, something that echoed within his own soul. "I'm here to listen," he said gently. "Whatever you have to say, I'll take it seriously."

She looked up at him, her eyes searching his face for any sign of deception. "Alright," she said finally, her voice trembling slightly. "It started about a year ago. I began hearing things... voices, memories... but they weren't mine. At first, I thought I was losing my mind. But then I realized that they were real—memories of people who had died, people I had never met."

Aaron's heart skipped a beat, the unease that had been gnawing at him all day suddenly intensifying. "Go on," he said, keeping his tone calm.

Elena took a deep breath, her hands clenching in her lap. "It's like... when I touch something that belonged to someone else, I can hear their thoughts, their memories. Sometimes it's just fragments, just bits and pieces. But other times... it's like I'm living their life, like I'm experiencing everything they went through."

Aaron's mind raced as he listened to her words. It was absurd, impossible, and yet... something about it rang true. He couldn't explain it, but he felt a connection to her story, a resonance that went beyond the clinical.

"I see," he said carefully. "And these echoes—how do they affect you? Do they cause you distress?"

Elena nodded, her eyes filling with tears. "Yes. They're overwhelming. I can't shut them out, no matter how hard I try. They invade my mind, my dreams... I can't escape them. And the worst part is, some of them are... dark. Terrible things that people have done, things they regret. It's like their guilt and pain become mine."

Aaron felt a shiver run down his spine. Her words struck a chord deep within him, stirring up memories he had long since buried. He could see the anguish in her eyes, the weight of the burden she carried, and he knew that it was real. She wasn't delusional, wasn't making it up. The echoes were real, and they were tormenting her in ways that he couldn't begin to understand.

"Ms. Carter," he said softly, his voice taking on a more compassionate tone, "I believe you. And I want to help you. We'll work together to find a way to manage these experiences, to help you regain control of your life."

Elena looked at him with a mixture of relief and disbelief. "You believe me?"

Aaron nodded. "Yes, I do. And I'm going to do everything I can to help you."

As he said the words, he felt a shift within himself, a crack in his facade that had grown too wide to ignore. For the first time in years, he felt a connection to a patient that went beyond the clinical, beyond the professional. He felt something he had long since forgotten—empathy, and with it, a sense of responsibility.

The session continued with Aaron asking Elena more about her experiences, gathering as much information as he could. But even as he focused on her, a part of his mind was turning inward, grappling with the implications of what she had told him.

The echoes were real. And if they were real for her, then they might be real for him too.

When the session finally ended, and Elena had left the office, Aaron sat alone in the silence, his thoughts swirling. He had spent his entire life trying to maintain control, to keep the chaos of his past at bay. But now, that control was slipping, and the cracks in his facade were growing wider with each passing moment.

And as he sat there, staring at the closed door, he couldn't shake the feeling that something had shifted, that his world had been irrevocably altered. The echoes of his past, and the echoes of Elena Carter's strange abilities, were drawing closer, and there was no telling what they might reveal when they finally broke through.

Aaron Blake was no longer in control, and the realization terrified him more than he cared to admit.

Chapter 2: Echoes of Darkness

The late afternoon sun cast long shadows across the walls of Dr. Aaron Blake's office, creating an atmosphere that was both serene and somber. The usual clinical precision of the room was softened by the golden light filtering through the half-drawn blinds, but there was an underlying tension that lingered in the air, an unspoken anticipation of what was to come.

Aaron sat behind his desk, his fingers drumming lightly on the polished surface as he reviewed the notes from his earlier session with Elena Carter. He had spent the last hour going over every detail, analyzing her words, her body language, and the strange unease that had settled over him during their conversation. There was something about Elena, something that defied explanation and gnawed at the edges of his mind, refusing to be dismissed.

He glanced at the clock on the wall—4:30 PM. Elena would be arriving for her first full session in a few minutes, and Aaron felt a flicker of apprehension, a rare emotion for him. He had always prided himself on his ability to remain detached, to approach every case with clinical precision. But Elena's case was different. Her claims, though outlandish, had struck a chord within him, stirring up memories and fears that he had long since buried.

He pushed those thoughts aside, forcing himself to focus. He needed to approach this session with the same level of professionalism he brought to every case, despite the growing unease that threatened to cloud his judgment. He had to maintain control, to keep the cracks in his facade from widening any further.

The door to his office opened, and Elena Carter stepped inside. She was dressed in a simple blouse and jeans, her dark hair pulled back into a loose ponytail. Her eyes, that unsettling shade of green, met his as she offered a tentative smile.

"Good afternoon, Ms. Carter," Aaron greeted her, rising from his chair and gesturing for her to take a seat. "Please, have a seat."

Elena nodded, her movements hesitant as she approached the chair across from his desk. She seemed smaller today, more fragile, as if the weight of the world had settled onto her shoulders. As she sat down, she clasped her hands in her lap, her fingers twisting together nervously.

"Thank you for seeing me again, Dr. Blake," she said, her voice soft but steady.

Aaron settled back into his chair, studying her with a practiced eye. "Of course, Ms. Carter. I've been reviewing the notes from our last meeting, and I'd like to delve deeper into some of the experiences you mentioned. I want to understand more about these echoes you've been hearing."

Elena's gaze dropped to her hands, her expression tightening. "I'm not sure where to start," she admitted. "It's... hard to explain. And I know it sounds crazy."

Aaron leaned forward slightly, his tone gentle. "You don't need to worry about that here. This is a safe space, and I'm here to listen, no matter how difficult it is to put into words. Just start wherever you feel comfortable."

Elena took a deep breath, her fingers stilling as she collected her thoughts. "It started about a year ago," she began, her voice barely above a whisper. "At first, it was just... small things. I would touch something—an object, a piece of clothing—and I would get these flashes. Images, sounds, feelings... but they weren't mine. They belonged to someone else, someone who had touched that object before."

Aaron listened intently, his skepticism tempered by genuine curiosity. He had encountered patients with similar claims before—individuals who believed they had psychic abilities, who heard voices or saw visions. In most cases, these symptoms were linked to underlying mental health conditions, such as schizophrenia or dissociative disorders. But Elena's account felt different, more vivid and detailed.

"Can you describe one of these experiences?" Aaron asked, keeping his voice neutral. "What exactly did you see or hear?"

Elena hesitated, her brow furrowing as she tried to recall a specific incident. "There was a necklace," she said slowly, her voice tinged with uncertainty. "It belonged to my grandmother. I found it in an old jewelry box after she passed away. When I picked it up, I... I felt something. It was like I was being pulled into her memories, but they were... distorted, fragmented. I saw her standing in front of a mirror, putting on the necklace, but the reflection in the mirror wasn't hers. It was someone else, someone I didn't recognize. And then I heard this voice, a man's voice, whispering her name."

Aaron's pen hovered over his notepad as he took in her words. The description was unsettlingly specific, and the way she recounted it suggested that it had left a deep impression on her. But the rational part of his mind still sought an explanation, a way to categorize her experiences within the framework of known psychological phenomena.

"Elena," he said carefully, "what you're describing could be related to a condition known as dissociation. It's a common symptom in individuals who have experienced trauma, where they feel disconnected from reality or from their own memories. Have you ever been diagnosed with PTSD or another dissociative disorder?"

Elena looked up at him, her eyes searching his face for something—validation, perhaps, or understanding. "I've been diagnosed with PTSD," she admitted. "It happened after... after an incident a few years ago. But this isn't like that. I know what dissociation feels like. This is different. It's like I'm being pulled into someone else's life, someone else's memories."

Aaron made a note of her response, his skepticism tempered by the sincerity in her voice. He had treated many patients with PTSD, individuals who had experienced unimaginable trauma and whose minds had fractured under the weight of those memories. Dissociation was a common coping mechanism, a way for the mind to protect itself from the full impact of the trauma. But Elena's description went beyond the typical symptoms he had encountered.

"Can you tell me more about the incident that led to your PTSD diagnosis?" Aaron asked, his tone gentle but probing. "It might help us understand how these experiences are connected."

Elena hesitated again, her expression tightening as she weighed whether or not to share something so deeply personal. Finally, she nodded, her voice trembling slightly as she spoke. "It was an accident," she began, her words measured and careful. "A car accident. I was driving with my younger sister, Emma. We were on our way home from a friend's house when a car ran a red light and hit us. Emma... she didn't make it."

Aaron felt a pang of sympathy as he listened to her story. The loss of a loved one in such a traumatic way could leave deep scars, scars that often manifested in the form of PTSD. But there was more to her story, something that still hadn't been fully revealed.

"I'm very sorry for your loss, Elena," Aaron said softly. "That kind of trauma can have a profound impact on the mind, and it's not uncommon for individuals to experience symptoms like flashbacks, nightmares, or even dissociation as a result. But you believe that what you're experiencing now is something different, something more than just a symptom of PTSD?"

Elena nodded, her eyes glistening with unshed tears. "Yes. The echoes... they didn't start right after the accident. It was months later, when I started going through Emma's things, packing up her room. That's when I started hearing the voices, seeing the images. But they weren't of the accident—they were of things that happened long before, things I couldn't possibly know about."

Aaron's curiosity deepened as he considered her words. The delayed onset of symptoms wasn't unusual in cases of PTSD, but the nature of those symptoms—the echoes, as she called them—didn't fit neatly into any category he was familiar with. It was as if her mind had become a conduit for memories and emotions that weren't her own, a phenomenon that defied logical explanation.

"Let's talk about these echoes in more detail," Aaron suggested, his tone still measured. "When you experience them, do you feel any physical sensations? Is there anything specific that triggers them?"

Elena seemed to relax slightly at the question, as if the shift to a more clinical discussion was a relief. "It's usually when I touch something that belonged to someone else," she explained. "An object, a piece of clothing, anything with a strong emotional connection to its owner. Sometimes it's just a fleeting feeling, like a whisper in the back of my mind. But other times... it's overwhelming. It's like I'm being pulled into their memories, living them as if they were my own."

Aaron made another note, his mind racing as he tried to process the information. The idea of objects carrying emotional imprints wasn't entirely foreign—there were theories in parapsychology about psychometry, the ability to read the history of an object by touching it. But those theories were on the fringes of science, dismissed by most mainstream psychologists as pseudoscience.

He cleared his throat, choosing his next words carefully. "Have you ever considered the possibility that these experiences might be influenced by your own memories and emotions? Our minds are incredibly complex, and it's not uncommon for people to project their own feelings onto the world around them, especially in the wake of a traumatic event."

Elena shook her head, her expression resolute. "I've thought about that, Dr. Blake. I've tried to rationalize it, to tell myself that it's just my mind playing tricks on me. But the things I see, the things I hear... they're too specific, too detailed. I know things about people I've never met

, things I couldn't possibly know."

Aaron leaned back in his chair, considering her words. There was no denying the intensity of her conviction, and yet his professional training urged him to remain skeptical. The mind was a powerful thing, capable of creating elaborate delusions and false memories, especially in individuals who had experienced severe trauma. But what if Elena's experiences were more than just the product of a fractured psyche? What if there was something else at play, something that he couldn't explain through the lens of psychology alone?

He hesitated for a moment, the words on the tip of his tongue. "Elena," he began slowly, "I want to help you find a way to manage these experiences, to regain control of your life. But to do that, we need to explore all possibilities, both psychological and... perhaps, other."

Elena looked up at him, her eyes widening slightly in surprise. "What do you mean, 'other'?"

Aaron felt a strange sense of vulnerability as he considered how to answer her. He had spent his entire career grounded in science, in the study of the mind and its complexities. But there were moments—fleeting, unbidden moments—when he questioned whether there were forces at work that went beyond the realm of science, forces that defied explanation.

"I mean that we need to keep an open mind," he said finally. "We'll explore the psychological aspects of what you're experiencing, but we'll also consider the possibility that there may be other factors at play, factors that we don't fully understand."

Elena seemed to relax at his words, as if the acknowledgment of the unknown was a comfort to her. "Thank you, Dr. Blake. I was afraid you wouldn't believe me, that you'd think I was crazy."

Aaron offered her a small, reassuring smile, though his own thoughts were far from settled. "I don't think you're crazy, Elena. I think you're dealing with something incredibly difficult, and it's my job to help you navigate it."

The session continued with Elena recounting more of her experiences with the echoes, each story more unsettling than the last. She spoke of touching an old photograph and hearing the desperate pleas of a man begging for forgiveness, of handling a locket and feeling the crushing sorrow of a woman who had lost her child. The details were vivid, too vivid to be dismissed as mere imagination.

As Aaron listened, he felt the unease within him growing, the cracks in his facade widening with each passing moment. He had always prided himself on his ability to remain detached, to approach every case with a clinical eye. But there was something about Elena's story that touched on the deepest recesses of his own mind, stirring up memories and fears that he had long since buried.

When the session finally drew to a close, Aaron felt a sense of relief, mixed with a lingering sense of dread. He had agreed to see Elena again, to continue exploring her experiences and searching for answers. But he couldn't shake the feeling that he was treading on dangerous ground, that he was opening himself up to forces that he didn't fully understand.

As Elena stood to leave, she hesitated, her hand resting on the edge of the desk. "Dr. Blake," she said quietly, her voice trembling slightly, "there's one more thing. Something I didn't mention before."

Aaron looked up at her, his brow furrowing in concern. "What is it, Elena?"

She hesitated, her eyes flickering with uncertainty. "I've been having dreams. Dreams about people I've never met, places I've never been. But they feel so real, like I'm living someone else's life. And sometimes... sometimes I think they're trying to tell me something, trying to warn me about something."

Aaron felt a chill run down his spine. The connection between dreams and the subconscious mind was well-documented in psychology, but Elena's description went beyond the typical manifestations of trauma or anxiety. It was as if her mind was reaching out, connecting with something—or someone—beyond her own experience.

"We'll explore that in our next session," Aaron said, his voice steady despite the unease that gripped him. "For now, try to keep a journal of your dreams, write down as much detail as you can remember. It might help us understand what's happening."

Elena nodded, her expression one of gratitude mixed with lingering fear. "Thank you, Dr. Blake. I'll do that."

As she turned to leave, her hand brushed against the edge of the desk, and something strange happened—something that neither of them could have anticipated.

The room seemed to shift, the air growing thick and heavy, as if time itself had slowed. Aaron felt a strange sensation, a tingling at the base of his skull, and then a flood of images, sounds, and emotions that weren't his own.

He saw a woman, young and beautiful, standing in a field of wildflowers, her face illuminated by the golden light of the setting sun. She was laughing, her eyes filled with joy, but there was a shadow behind her, something dark and menacing that crept closer with each passing moment. The woman's laughter turned to a scream, and then the scene shifted, replaced by the sound of shattering glass and the cold, metallic scent of blood.

Aaron gasped, his hand clutching the edge of the desk as the vision faded, leaving him disoriented and shaken. He looked up to see Elena staring at him, her eyes wide with shock.

"Did you... did you feel that?" she asked, her voice barely above a whisper.

Aaron struggled to find his voice, his mind reeling from the intensity of the experience. "I... I don't know what that was," he admitted, his voice trembling.

Elena's eyes filled with tears, her hands shaking as she clasped them to her chest. "I'm so sorry, Dr. Blake. I didn't mean to... I didn't know it could happen to someone else."

Aaron forced himself to take a deep breath, to regain some semblance of control. "It's alright, Elena. We'll figure this out together."

But even as he spoke the words, he knew that something had changed, something fundamental that went beyond the boundaries of his understanding. The echoes were real, and they had touched him in a way that he couldn't explain.

As Elena left the office, Aaron remained seated at his desk, staring at the spot where she had stood, his mind racing. The cracks in his facade had widened, and the control he had fought so hard to maintain was slipping through his fingers.

He was no longer just an observer in Elena's story—he was now a participant, drawn into a world of echoes and memories that defied explanation.

And as he sat there, alone in the gathering darkness, Aaron Blake realized that he was standing on the edge of something far more terrifying than he had ever imagined.

Chapter 3: The Dark Within

The old house loomed ahead of Aaron Blake, a silhouette against the darkening sky, its edges blurred by time and neglect. The once stately Victorian home, nestled on the outskirts of a small, now forgotten town, had long since fallen into disrepair. The windows were boarded up, the paint peeling in long strips, and the overgrown garden had swallowed the front path whole. Yet, despite the years of abandonment, the house still stood—a monument to the past, to memories both cherished and dreaded.

Aaron parked his car at the end of the gravel driveway, the tires crunching over stones as he came to a stop. The engine's hum faded into silence, and he sat there for a moment, staring at the house that had once been his home. His hands gripped the steering wheel tightly, knuckles white, as he fought the urge to simply turn around and leave. But he knew he couldn't. Not now, not after everything that had happened.

The echoes that had begun to infiltrate his life—Elena's life—had stirred something deep within him, something that had been dormant for years. Memories he had tried to forget, emotions he had buried. They were all surfacing now, like shadows creeping out of the corners of his mind. And he knew, with a certainty that both terrified and compelled him, that the answers he sought lay within the walls of this old, decaying house.

With a deep breath, Aaron unclenched his hands and opened the car door. The evening air was cool, carrying with it the faint scent of earth and decaying leaves. He stepped out, the gravel shifting beneath his feet as he approached the house. Each step was heavy, laden with the weight of the past, and the closer he got, the more the unease in his chest grew.

The front door, once a vibrant shade of red, was now faded and chipped, hanging slightly askew on its hinges. Aaron reached out and pushed it open, the wood creaking in protest as it swung inward, revealing the dark interior beyond. He hesitated on the threshold, his breath catching in his throat as he was hit with a wave of nostalgia—a potent mixture of longing and dread.

Stepping inside, he was greeted by the scent of dust and damp wood, a smell that brought with it a flood of memories. The grand foyer, once immaculate and filled with the sound of his mother's laughter, was now a shadow of its former self. The chandelier that had once hung from the ceiling was gone, replaced by a single, bare bulb that cast a weak, flickering light. The walls, lined with faded wallpaper, were cracked and peeling, revealing the bare wood beneath.

Aaron's footsteps echoed through the empty halls as he made his way deeper into the house. The silence was oppressive, broken only by the creak of the floorboards beneath his feet and the occasional rustle of a small creature scurrying through the walls. Every sound seemed amplified in the stillness, each one sending a shiver down his spine.

He walked past the parlor, the dining room, the kitchen—each one a snapshot of a life long gone, frozen in time by the decay that had set in. But it was the study that drew him, the room at the end of the hall, the place where his father had spent most of his time. Richard Blake had been a man of science, a renowned psychiatrist who had dedicated his life to understanding the human mind. But he had also been a man of secrets, and it was those secrets that had ultimately consumed him.

The door to the study was closed, the brass handle tarnished and cold to the touch. Aaron hesitated for a moment, his hand hovering over the handle as he fought the urge to turn back. But he knew he couldn't. He had come this far, and whatever lay beyond this door, he needed to confront it.

With a deep breath, he turned the handle and pushed the door open.

The study was exactly as he remembered it—dark, cluttered, and filled with the scent of old books and leather. The heavy drapes were drawn, allowing only a sliver of the dying light to filter through, casting long shadows across the room. The walls were lined with bookshelves, each one crammed with volumes on psychiatry, neurology, and the occult. In the center of the room stood a large oak desk, its surface covered with papers, journals, and medical instruments, all left exactly as they had been the last time his father had sat there.

Aaron stepped inside, the door creaking shut behind him, sealing him in with the ghosts of his past. He felt a chill run down his spine as he surveyed the room, the weight of the years pressing down on him. This was the heart of the house, the place where his father had conducted his most important work, and where he had kept his darkest secrets.

As a child, Aaron had been forbidden from entering the study. It was his father's sanctuary, a place where he could retreat from the world and lose himself in his research. But now, standing in the room that had once been off-limits, Aaron felt a strange sense of both reverence and dread. This was the place where his father had unlocked the mysteries of the mind, where he had conducted experiments that had pushed the boundaries of ethics and science. And it was here, Aaron knew, that he would find the answers he sought.

He approached the desk, his fingers brushing lightly over the surface as he scanned the papers that were scattered across it. They were filled with his father's meticulous handwriting—notes on patient cases, sketches of brain anatomy, and pages upon pages of observations on the nature of consciousness. But there was something else, something hidden beneath the layers of medical jargon and scientific analysis—something darker.

Aaron pulled out the chair and sat down, the leather creaking beneath his weight. He reached for one of the journals, a thick, leather-bound volume that seemed older than the others. The cover was worn, the edges frayed, and the pages were yellowed with age. As he opened it, he was hit with the faint scent of old paper, and something else—a hint of something metallic, like blood.

The journal was filled with detailed notes, charts, and diagrams, all written in his father's familiar script. But as Aaron read through the entries, a sense of unease began to settle over him. The notes were different from the ones he had seen in his father's other journals—these were more personal, more chaotic, as if they had been written in a fevered state. The handwriting was uneven, the letters slanting and sprawling across the page, and the content was disturbing.

Richard Blake had been researching the nature of memory, specifically the way trauma could fragment and distort it. He had been particularly interested in the phenomenon of repressed memories, and how they could be accessed and manipulated. But as Aaron read further, he realized that his father's research had taken a darker turn. He had begun to experiment on his patients, using techniques that were both unethical and dangerous.

There were references to procedures that involved inducing dissociation, fragmenting the mind to uncover hidden memories. Richard had used drugs, hypnosis, and sensory deprivation to push his patients to the brink, to break down the barriers between the conscious and unconscious mind. He had believed that by doing so, he could unlock the deepest recesses of the psyche, revealing the truth buried within.

But the results had been disastrous.

Aaron's hands shook as he turned the pages, his heart pounding in his chest. The journal detailed the effects of the experiments—patients who had been left catatonic, others who had developed severe psychosis, and some who had simply disappeared. The entries became more and more erratic as his father's descent into obsession deepened, his notes filled with frantic scribbles about "the echoes" and "the darkness within."

Aaron stopped on a page where the handwriting had become almost illegible, the words scrawled across the page in a frenzy. It was an entry that detailed his father's final experiment, one that he had conducted on himself. Richard Blake had believed that by turning his methods inward, by subjecting himself to the same procedures he had used on his patients, he could access a part of his own mind that had been hidden from him—an echo of something dark, something that had been haunting him for years.

The entry ended abruptly, the last few lines trailing off into incoherence. There was no record of what had happened during that final experiment, no explanation of the results. But Aaron knew, deep down, that whatever his father had uncovered, it had driven him to the brink of madness.

Aaron closed the journal, his breath coming in short, shallow gasps. The room seemed to close in around him, the shadows pressing in from all sides. He felt as if he were on the edge of a precipice, staring into an abyss that threatened to swallow him whole. The secrets his father had kept, the darkness he had uncovered—it was all too much, too overwhelming.

But Aaron couldn't turn back now. He had to know the truth, no matter how horrifying it might be.

He stood up, his legs trembling as he crossed the room to the bookshelves that lined the walls. He ran his fingers along the spines of the books, searching for something—anything—that might give him more insight into his father's work. And then, his hand stopped on a book that was different from the others, its cover plain and unmarked.

Aaron pulled the book from the shelf, his fingers trembling as he opened it. Inside, he found more of his father's notes, but these were different—more cryptic, filled with symbols and references to the occult. There were sketches of rituals, diagrams of sigils, and notes on ancient texts that spoke of spirits, echoes, and the manipulation of the soul.

The further Aaron read,

the more disturbed he became. His father hadn't just been experimenting with the mind—he had been delving into something far darker, something that went beyond the boundaries of science. Richard Blake had been trying to access a part of the human soul, to tap into a force that was both ancient and malevolent. And in doing so, he had unleashed something that he couldn't control.

Aaron's hands shook as he closed the book, his mind racing. The echoes that Elena had described, the voices and memories that weren't her own—it was all connected. His father had uncovered something dark, something that had been passed down to him, something that was now threatening to consume him.

He turned to leave the study, but as he did, his foot caught on something beneath the desk. He looked down and saw a small, metal box, half-hidden beneath a pile of old papers. He reached down and pulled it out, his fingers fumbling with the latch. Inside, he found a series of old photographs, each one depicting a different patient—patients who had been subjected to his father's experiments.

The faces in the photographs were haunting, their eyes vacant and hollow, as if the life had been drained from them. Aaron felt a shiver run down his spine as he recognized one of the faces—it was a man he had seen before, in one of the echoes that had haunted him since his last session with Elena. The man's eyes were filled with terror, his mouth open in a silent scream.

Aaron dropped the box, the photographs scattering across the floor. He staggered back, his heart pounding in his chest. The darkness that his father had uncovered, the echoes that had begun to infiltrate his life—it was all connected, all part of a legacy that he had inherited.

He had to get out of the house, had to escape the shadows that threatened to consume him. But as he turned to leave, he felt a cold hand on his shoulder, and the room seemed to tilt, the walls closing in around him.

Aaron gasped, his vision blurring as he felt himself being pulled into the darkness. The echoes were all around him, whispering in his ears, filling his mind with memories that weren't his own. He saw flashes of his father's face, twisted in agony, heard the sound of his mother's laughter turning into a scream, and felt the weight of the past pressing down on him, crushing him beneath its weight.

And then, everything went black.

AARON AWOKE TO DARKNESS, the cold floor beneath him sending a shiver through his body. For a moment, he was disoriented, his mind struggling to piece together where he was and how he had gotten there. But then, the memories came flooding back—the house, the study, the echoes that had overwhelmed him.

He pushed himself up, his body aching as he tried to steady himself. The room was dark, the only light coming from a sliver of moonlight that filtered through the crack in the drapes. The photographs were scattered across the floor, the faces staring up at him, their eyes vacant and hollow.

Aaron took a deep breath, trying to calm the panic that threatened to overtake him. He had to get out of here, had to leave the house before the darkness consumed him completely. But as he stood up, he felt something cold and wet beneath his hand.

He looked down and saw that his hand was covered in blood—fresh, warm blood. His heart skipped a beat as he realized that the blood was coming from his own body, from a deep gash on his arm that he hadn't noticed before.

Aaron staggered to the door, his vision swimming as he fumbled with the handle. He had to get out, had to escape the shadows that were closing in around him. But as he opened the door, he felt a cold breeze wash over him, and the echoes came rushing back, filling his mind with memories that weren't his own.

He saw his father, standing in the study, his eyes wide with terror as he held the same metal box that Aaron had found. Richard Blake was mumbling to himself, his words incoherent, his hands shaking as he flipped through the photographs. And then, suddenly, he screamed—a blood-curdling scream that echoed through the house, reverberating off the walls.

Aaron stumbled back, his heart racing as he tried to shake off the vision. But it was too late. The echoes were all around him, whispering in his ears, filling his mind with darkness. He could feel them pressing down on him, suffocating him, dragging him down into the abyss.

With a last burst of strength, Aaron pushed himself out of the study and into the hallway. The house seemed to warp around him, the walls closing in, the shadows twisting and writhing. He could hear his father's voice, could feel his presence, and knew that the darkness that had consumed Richard Blake was now coming for him.

Aaron ran, his feet slipping on the blood-slicked floor as he stumbled through the house. He didn't know where he was going, didn't care. He just had to get out, had to escape before the darkness swallowed him whole.

He burst through the front door, the cool night air hitting him like a slap in the face. He gasped, his lungs burning as he sucked in the fresh air. But even as he stood on the front porch, his body trembling, he could feel the echoes lingering in his mind, could hear their whispers in the back of his mind.

Aaron staggered to his car, his vision blurring as he fumbled with the keys. He had to get away, had to escape the shadows that had followed him from the house. But as he started the engine and pulled away from the house, he knew that it was too late.

The darkness that his father had uncovered, the echoes that had begun to infiltrate his life—they were now a part of him, a shadow that he couldn't escape. And as he drove away from the house, leaving it behind in the darkness, he knew that his life would never be the same.

Chapter 4: Into the Abyss

The apartment was a reflection of its occupant's mind—a chaotic maze of clutter, shadows, and silence. It was a small space, barely enough room for the essentials, but every inch of it seemed to be filled with something: books piled high on every available surface, clothes strewn across the floor, and canvases leaning haphazardly against the walls, each one a window into a world of darkness and turmoil.

Elena Carter sat in the middle of it all, cross-legged on the floor, surrounded by her drawings. Her dark hair fell in tangled strands around her pale face, her green eyes fixed on the sketchpad in front of her. The room was silent, save for the faint scratching of her pencil as it moved across the paper, tracing lines that seemed to flow from some unseen place deep within her mind.

She had been drawing for hours, losing herself in the intricate patterns and images that emerged from the tip of her pencil. It was the only thing that kept the echoes at bay, the only thing that gave her a sense of control in a world that had become increasingly chaotic and terrifying. But even as she poured her fears and nightmares onto the paper, she knew it was only a temporary reprieve. The echoes were always there, lurking in the shadows, waiting for a moment of weakness to break through.

Elena paused, her hand trembling slightly as she looked down at the drawing she had just completed. It was a dark, twisted image—an old, crumbling asylum, its windows shattered, its walls covered in strange, cryptic symbols. In the foreground stood a figure, half-shrouded in shadow, its face obscured, but its eyes—those haunting, hollow eyes—stared back at her with a look of indescribable sorrow and pain.

She didn't know where the image had come from, but it was familiar in a way that made her stomach churn. It was as if she had seen it before, in a dream, or perhaps in one of the echoes that had invaded her mind. She couldn't be sure anymore. The line between her own thoughts and the memories of others had become so blurred that she no longer knew what was real and what was not.

With a sigh, Elena set the sketchpad aside and rose to her feet, the room spinning slightly as she stood. She hadn't eaten all day, hadn't slept in what felt like weeks. The exhaustion weighed heavily on her, a physical and emotional burden that she could no longer carry. But the thought of sleep terrified her. That was when the echoes were at their worst, when they invaded her dreams and turned them into nightmares that left her waking in a cold sweat, her heart racing, her mind on the verge of collapse.

She stumbled to the kitchen, her bare feet shuffling over the cold tile floor. The kitchen was just as cluttered as the rest of the apartment—dishes piled in the sink, empty food containers littering the counter, and a half-empty bottle of wine sitting on the table. She reached for the bottle, her hand trembling as she poured the remaining liquid into a glass. It wasn't much, but it would take the edge off, dull the fear that gnawed at her insides.

As she lifted the glass to her lips, a sudden noise made her freeze—a faint whisper, like the sound of someone murmuring just out of earshot. She set the glass down, her heart pounding as she strained to listen. The apartment was silent, the only sound the soft hum of the refrigerator. But the whispering persisted, growing louder, more insistent, until it was all she could hear.

Elena squeezed her eyes shut, pressing her hands to her ears in a desperate attempt to block out the sound. But it was no use. The echoes were too strong, too deeply embedded in her mind. They were like parasites, feeding on her fear, her guilt, her sorrow, until there was nothing left but darkness.

"Stop it," she whispered, her voice trembling. "Please, just stop."

But the echoes didn't stop. They never did.

The memories flooded her mind, a torrent of images and emotions that weren't her own. She saw a young woman standing on a bridge, her eyes filled with tears as she looked down at the rushing water below. She felt the woman's despair, her hopelessness, her overwhelming guilt. And then, without warning, the woman stepped forward, her body plummeting into the icy water below, her scream swallowed by the night.

Elena gasped, her eyes snapping open as the vision faded, leaving her trembling and breathless. She knew that the memory she had just experienced wasn't hers, but it felt so real, so vivid, that it was as if she had lived it herself. The echoes were becoming more intense, more invasive, and she was powerless to stop them.

She reached for the glass of wine, her hand shaking so badly that she nearly knocked it over. The liquid burned as it went down, but it did little to quell the fear that had taken root in her chest. She was losing herself, being consumed by the memories of others, until there was nothing left of her own identity. She was becoming a vessel, a conduit for the echoes, and it terrified her more than anything she had ever experienced.

Elena stumbled back to the living room, her legs barely able to support her. She collapsed onto the couch, her head falling into her hands as she tried to steady her breathing. But the fear, the despair—it was all too much. The darkness was closing in, and she didn't know how much longer she could fight it.

Her eyes fell on the sketchpad lying on the floor, the image of the asylum staring back at her with those hollow, empty eyes. She didn't want to look at it, didn't want to acknowledge the truth that it represented. But she couldn't turn away. The drawing called to her, pulled her in, until she couldn't resist its dark allure.

With trembling hands, she picked up the sketchpad and flipped through the pages, each one more disturbing than the last. There were images of places she had never been, people she had never met, but they all felt so familiar, so real. It was as if she had seen them before, in another life, or perhaps in the echoes that haunted her.

One drawing, in particular, caught her eye. It was a simple sketch, rough and unrefined, but it sent a chill down her spine. It depicted a man standing in a dark hallway, his face obscured by shadow, but his posture tense, as if he were listening for something just out of sight. In the background, barely visible, was the faint outline of a door, cracked open just enough to reveal a sliver of light.

Elena stared at the drawing, her heart pounding in her chest. She didn't remember drawing it, didn't know where the image had come from, but it filled her with a sense of dread that she couldn't shake. The man in the drawing—there was something about him, something familiar. But she couldn't place it, couldn't remember where she had seen him before.

Her breath quickened as she flipped to the next page, her eyes widening as she took in the image before her. It was the same man, but this time he was standing in a room filled with medical equipment—an old, dusty room that looked like it hadn't been used in years. The walls were lined with shelves, each one filled with jars and vials, and in the center of the room was a table, upon which lay a body, covered with a white sheet.

Elena felt a wave of nausea wash over her as she stared at the drawing. She didn't know how she knew it, but she was certain that the man in the drawing was her father. And the room—she had never seen it before, but it felt so familiar, as if she had been there in another life, or perhaps in one of the echoes that had invaded her mind.

A sob escaped her lips as she dropped the sketchpad, her hands trembling uncontrollably. She couldn't do this anymore. She couldn't keep fighting the darkness that was consuming her, the memories that weren't her own, the guilt that was slowly eating away at her soul. She was losing herself, becoming a vessel for the echoes, and she didn't know how to stop it.

In a moment of desperation, Elena reached for her phone and dialed the number she had memorized from her last visit to Dr. Blake's office. She didn't know what she would say, didn't even know if he could help her, but she couldn't do this alone. She needed someone to anchor her to reality, someone to pull her back from the brink of madness.

The phone rang once, twice, and then she heard his voice—calm, measured, the voice of a man who was always in control.

"Dr. Blake," Aaron answered, his tone professional but tinged with concern. "Elena, is that you?"

Elena swallowed hard, her voice trembling as she spoke. "Dr. Blake, I... I need help. I can't... I can't do this anymore."

There was a pause on the other end of the line, and then Aaron's voice softened. "Elena, take a deep breath. Tell me what's going on."

She tried to steady her breathing, tried to find the words to explain the chaos that had consumed her life, but all she could manage was a choked sob. "The echoes... they're getting worse. I can't control them. I can't... I can't stop them."

"Elena, listen to me," Aaron said, his voice firm but gentle. "You're not alone in this. I'm here to help you. But I need you to stay with me, okay? Can you do that?"

She nodded

, even though he couldn't see her. "Okay," she whispered, her voice barely audible.

"Good," Aaron said. "Now, I want you to tell me what's been happening. Start from the beginning."

Elena took a shaky breath and began to talk, the words spilling out of her like a torrent. She told him about the echoes, the memories that weren't hers, the drawings that seemed to come from some dark place deep within her mind. She told him about the dreams, the visions of her father, and the overwhelming guilt that had consumed her since the accident.

Aaron listened in silence, his expression unreadable as he absorbed everything she said. But inside, his mind was racing, trying to make sense of the connections between her experiences, the echoes, and the darkness that seemed to be closing in around both of them.

"Elena," he said after she had finished, his voice measured and calm, "I'm going to help you through this. But I need you to trust me. Can you do that?"

"Yes," Elena whispered, her voice trembling. "I trust you."

"Good," Aaron said. "I want you to take some time tonight to rest. Try to get some sleep, if you can. We'll meet tomorrow, and we'll work through this together."

Elena nodded, even though the thought of sleep terrified her. "Okay," she said, her voice barely audible.

"And Elena," Aaron added, his voice softening, "you're not alone in this. Remember that."

Tears welled up in Elena's eyes as she clutched the phone to her chest. "Thank you, Dr. Blake," she whispered. "Thank you."

They ended the call, and Elena sat in the silence of her apartment, the weight of the conversation heavy on her shoulders. She knew that Aaron was trying to help, that he was the only person who seemed to understand what she was going through. But the darkness that surrounded her, the echoes that haunted her—it was all too much, too overwhelming.

She stared down at the sketchpad lying on the floor, the images she had drawn staring back at her with hollow, empty eyes. She didn't know where the drawings had come from, didn't know if they were memories or visions or something else entirely. But she knew one thing for certain—whatever they were, they were a reflection of the darkness that had taken hold of her soul.

With a heavy sigh, Elena picked up the sketchpad and flipped to a blank page. She didn't want to draw, didn't want to give life to the images that haunted her mind. But she couldn't stop herself. It was the only thing that gave her a sense of control, the only thing that kept the echoes at bay.

She picked up the pencil, her hand trembling as she began to draw. The lines flowed from her fingertips, dark and twisted, forming shapes and images that seemed to come from some deep, hidden place within her mind. She didn't know what she was drawing, didn't know what the image would be, but she couldn't stop. It was as if the pencil had a life of its own, moving across the paper with a will that wasn't hers.

When she finally stopped, her hand aching, her breath coming in short, shallow gasps, she stared down at the drawing in front of her. It was a disturbing image—dark, twisted, and filled with shadows. But there, in the center of it all, was a figure, standing alone in the darkness, surrounded by a swirling vortex of echoes and memories.

Elena dropped the pencil, her heart pounding in her chest. The figure in the drawing—it was her. She was the one standing in the darkness, surrounded by the echoes that threatened to consume her. She was the one who was losing herself, being pulled into a world of shadows and memories that weren't her own.

She pushed the sketchpad away, unable to look at it any longer. The drawing was too real, too close to the truth that she didn't want to acknowledge. The darkness that surrounded her, the echoes that haunted her—it was all consuming her, piece by piece, until there was nothing left.

Elena curled up on the couch, pulling a blanket over herself as she tried to block out the world around her. She felt so alone, so lost, trapped in a nightmare that she couldn't escape. And the worst part was, she didn't know if she even wanted to escape. The darkness had become a part of her, a reflection of the guilt and sorrow that had consumed her soul.

As she closed her eyes, tears streaming down her face, she could still hear the echoes, whispering in the back of her mind, filling her with memories that weren't hers. And in that moment, she knew that the darkness would never leave her. It was a part of her now, a shadow that would follow her wherever she went.

But as she drifted off into a fitful sleep, one thought lingered in the back of her mind—a faint glimmer of hope that maybe, just maybe, Dr. Blake could help her find a way out of the darkness.

Chapter 5: The Thin Veil

Detective Mark Harris had seen more than his share of darkness during his years on the force. He had investigated murders, drug rings, and domestic violence cases that left scars on his psyche, but nothing had ever shaken him quite like the cases he was now confronted with. The town of Greystone, once a sleepy haven where nothing more severe than a petty theft marred the police blotter, had been gripped by a series of strange and unsettling incidents that defied explanation.

The police station, normally a place of dull routine, was now buzzing with a tension that seemed to creep into the corners of the old building. Mark sat at his desk, surrounded by stacks of reports and photographs, each one more disturbing than the last. His partner, Detective Rachel Moore, was pacing the floor, her brow furrowed in concentration as she reviewed the latest case file.

Mark ran a hand through his graying hair, his eyes narrowing as he focused on the photograph in front of him. It was a picture of a man in his late fifties, found dead in his own home just a week ago. The cause of death had been ruled as a heart attack, but the circumstances surrounding it were anything but ordinary. The man had been a former patient at Greystone Asylum, the now-defunct psychiatric hospital on the outskirts of town, and his body had been discovered in a state of absolute terror. His face, frozen in a rictus of fear, haunted Mark even now.

"What do you make of it?" Rachel's voice broke through his thoughts, and Mark looked up to see her standing beside his desk, arms crossed, a skeptical look on her face.

Mark sighed, leaning back in his chair. "I don't know. It doesn't add up. We've got three dead, all former patients of Greystone Asylum, all found in similar conditions—scared out of their minds. But no signs of a struggle, no evidence of foul play."

Rachel nodded, her expression grim. "And then there are the ones who are still alive. Those who've been reporting strange sightings, hearing voices, experiencing things that just don't make any sense. It's like something's haunting them."

Mark frowned, drumming his fingers on the desk. He had never been one to entertain thoughts of the supernatural, preferring to rely on facts, evidence, and reason. But the more he delved into these cases, the more he was confronted with the possibility that something far beyond his understanding was at work.

"Have you heard from the coroner's office?" Mark asked, flipping through the pages of the file.

Rachel shook her head. "Not yet. But I don't expect them to find anything new. These deaths... they're not normal, Mark. And I don't think we're going to get any answers from the usual channels."

Mark grunted in agreement, his mind racing as he tried to piece together the fragments of information they had gathered. The town's history was steeped in whispers of dark secrets, of strange occurrences that had been buried beneath the veneer of normalcy. Greystone Asylum had been at the center of many of those whispers, a place where the town's unwanted had been sent to be forgotten, their stories left to fester in the shadows.

Mark had grown up in Greystone, had heard the tales of the asylum's dark past—of patients who had disappeared, of doctors who had dabbled in things best left alone. But like most of the townspeople, he had dismissed them as just that—stories, the kind that parents told their children to keep them from wandering too far from home.

Now, though, as he sat in his office surrounded by evidence that defied explanation, he couldn't help but wonder if there was more truth to those stories than he had ever believed.

"Have you ever looked into the asylum's history?" Mark asked, glancing up at Rachel. "I mean, really looked into it?"

Rachel raised an eyebrow. "You think the asylum has something to do with this?"

Mark shrugged. "I don't know. But it's a connection, and it's the only one we've got. These people—every one of them has ties to that place. Maybe there's something there, something we've missed."

Rachel was silent for a moment, considering his words. "You might be right," she said finally. "There were always rumors about that place, about the experiments they conducted on the patients. But it was all so long ago... I don't know how much we'll be able to dig up."

Mark nodded, knowing she was right. The asylum had been shut down decades ago, its records sealed, its history buried beneath layers of bureaucracy. But he also knew that the town had a way of keeping its secrets, and if there was something to be found, he would find it.

"I'm going to pay a visit to the archives," Mark said, pushing back his chair and standing up. "See if I can dig up anything on the asylum, or on these patients. Maybe there's something in their histories that can give us a clue."

Rachel nodded. "I'll see if I can track down any living relatives, anyone who might have more information. And I'll keep an eye on the new reports coming in. If there's a pattern, we'll find it."

Mark grabbed his coat and made his way out of the station, his mind already turning over the possibilities. The late afternoon sun was beginning to dip below the horizon, casting long shadows across the streets as he headed toward the town's archives. The wind had picked up, carrying with it the scent of autumn leaves and something else—something musty, like the smell of old books and forgotten places.

The archives were housed in a small, nondescript building on the edge of town, a place that most of the townspeople had forgotten even existed. It was a relic of another time, a place where the town's history had been preserved, though few cared to remember it. The building was old, the bricks weathered and cracked, the windows covered in a fine layer of dust.

Mark pushed open the heavy wooden door and stepped inside, the scent of dust and paper hitting him like a wall. The interior was dimly lit, the only sound the soft hum of the overhead lights. Rows of shelves stretched out before him, each one filled with boxes and binders, the records of the town's past.

He approached the front desk, where an elderly woman sat, peering at him through thick glasses. Her hair was pulled back in a tight bun, and she wore a cardigan that looked as old as the building itself.

"Detective Harris," he said, offering her a polite nod. "I'm looking for any records you might have on Greystone Asylum. Patients, doctors, anything from the time it was in operation."

The woman blinked at him, her expression one of mild surprise. "Greystone Asylum? My, that's going back quite a ways. Haven't had anyone ask about that place in years."

Mark offered her a thin smile. "I'm hoping you might still have some records. Anything you can find would be helpful."

The woman nodded slowly, pushing her chair back and standing with some effort. "Follow me, then. The records you're looking for would be in the back, under the special collections."

Mark followed her through the maze of shelves, the dim light casting long shadows on the walls. The air grew cooler as they walked, and he could feel the weight of history pressing down on him, the silent presence of the past lingering in the air.

They reached the back of the archives, where the woman led him to a small, locked door. She pulled out a key from the chain around her neck and unlocked it, revealing a narrow room lined with shelves, each one filled with boxes labeled with dates and names.

"These are the records from the asylum," she said, her voice echoing in the small space. "They've been here for years, untouched for the most part. You're welcome to take a look, but I'm afraid they might not be in the best condition."

Mark nodded, stepping into the room and taking in the sight of the boxes stacked neatly on the shelves. The labels were faded, the ink smudged with age, but he could still make out the dates—some going back nearly a century.

"Thank you," he said, turning to the woman. "This is exactly what I need."

She gave him a nod and shuffled back to the front of the archives, leaving Mark alone in the small room. He pulled out one of the boxes, the cardboard soft and brittle beneath his fingers, and set it on the small table in the center of the room.

Opening the box, he found a collection of old files, each one yellowed with age and covered in a thin layer of dust. The names of former patients were scrawled across the top of each file, along with dates of admission and discharge. Mark began to sift through the files, his eyes scanning the pages for anything that might stand out.

The further he dug, the more he realized just how extensive the asylum's history was. Patients had been admitted for a wide range of conditions—schizophrenia, depression, hysteria, and more. But there were also records of more unusual cases, patients who had been admitted for reasons that were vague and poorly documented. Some of the files mentioned experiments, procedures that were classified as "advanced treatments," though there was little detail about what those treatments entailed.

One file in particular caught his attention. It was thicker than the others, the name on the front barely legible—*Richard Blake*. Mark's heart skipped a beat. He had heard the name before, though he couldn't immediately place it. He opened the file, his eyes narrowing as he began to read.

Richard Blake had been one of the asylum's leading doctors, a

man known for his pioneering work in the field of psychiatry. But as Mark read further, it became clear that Blake's work had taken a dark turn. The file contained notes on a series of experiments Blake had conducted, experiments that involved memory manipulation, dissociation, and the study of what Blake referred to as "echoes."

Mark's pulse quickened as he read through the notes, his mind racing. The term "echoes" was one that had come up in some of the recent reports from the surviving patients, individuals who claimed to hear voices or see visions that weren't their own. Blake's notes were filled with references to these echoes, describing them as remnants of the past, memories that had somehow become detached from their original owners and now haunted those who were sensitive to them.

The further Mark read, the more disturbing the notes became. Blake had been obsessed with the idea of unlocking the hidden recesses of the mind, of tapping into a collective consciousness that transcended time and space. He had conducted experiments on his patients, pushing them to the brink of madness in his quest to understand the echoes.

And then, without warning, the notes stopped. There was no record of what had happened to Blake or the patients he had experimented on. The file ended abruptly, as if the story had been cut off before it could be completed.

Mark leaned back in his chair, his mind reeling from what he had just read. The echoes, the strange incidents in town—they were all connected to the asylum, to Richard Blake's experiments. And if Blake's notes were to be believed, the echoes were real, remnants of the past that had somehow taken on a life of their own.

But what did it all mean? And how was it connected to the deaths of the former patients?

Mark closed the file, his hands trembling slightly. He needed more information, needed to understand what had happened to Blake and his patients. And there was only one person who might have the answers.

Aaron Blake.

Mark had heard the name before, knew that Aaron was a well-respected psychiatrist who had followed in his father's footsteps. But if Richard Blake had been involved in such dark and twisted experiments, there was a chance that Aaron knew more than he was letting on.

Mark made his way back to the front of the archives, where the elderly woman was waiting for him.

"Did you find what you were looking for?" she asked, her voice tinged with curiosity.

"I did," Mark replied, trying to keep his tone neutral. "Thank you for your help."

She nodded, watching him with a keen eye as he left the building. The sun had dipped below the horizon by the time he stepped outside, the sky darkening as the first stars began to appear.

Mark's mind was racing as he made his way back to the station. He needed to talk to Aaron, needed to understand what his father had been involved in and how it was connected to the strange incidents in town. But he also knew that he had to tread carefully. If Aaron was hiding something, he wouldn't be willing to give up the truth easily.

The drive back to the station was a blur, Mark's thoughts consumed by the file he had just read. The town's dark history, the echoes, the strange deaths—it was all connected, and he was determined to uncover the truth, no matter how deep the darkness went.

When he arrived back at the station, Rachel was waiting for him, a grim expression on her face.

"What did you find?" she asked as he walked in.

Mark handed her the file on Richard Blake, watching as she flipped through the pages, her eyes widening as she read.

"This is... this is disturbing," she said finally, looking up at him. "You think Aaron Blake knows something?"

Mark nodded. "I do. His father was involved in some pretty dark stuff, and if anyone knows what's going on, it's him. I'm going to talk to him, see what he has to say."

Rachel frowned, closing the file and handing it back to him. "Be careful, Mark. If what's in that file is true, then we're dealing with something way out of our league."

Mark gave her a tight smile. "Don't worry, Rachel. I've dealt with plenty of darkness in my time. I can handle this."

But even as he said the words, he couldn't shake the feeling that this was different, that he was dealing with something far more sinister than he had ever encountered before.

As he left the station, his thoughts were consumed by the task ahead. He had to get to the bottom of this, had to uncover the truth about the echoes and the dark legacy of Richard Blake. And to do that, he would have to confront Aaron Blake, a man who might hold the key to unraveling the mystery that had gripped the town.

The night was dark as Mark drove through the quiet streets of Greystone, the weight of the file on Richard Blake sitting heavily in his lap. The shadows seemed to stretch out, reaching for him as he drove, as if the darkness itself was alive, watching, waiting.

He couldn't shake the feeling that he was being drawn into something far larger, something that went beyond the mundane world of police work and into the realm of the supernatural. The echoes, the strange incidents, the deaths—it was all connected, and the deeper he dug, the more he realized that the veil between the living and the dead was thinner than he had ever imagined.

As he approached Aaron Blake's house, Mark felt a chill run down his spine. He had faced down killers, had walked into crime scenes that would haunt him for the rest of his life, but this felt different. The darkness he was facing now was intangible, a force that couldn't be fought with bullets or handcuffs.

But Mark was determined. He would find the truth, no matter the cost.

He pulled up to the house, his eyes narrowing as he took in the darkened windows, the silence that hung over the property like a shroud. He stepped out of the car, the cold night air biting at his skin as he approached the front door.

Mark took a deep breath, steeling himself for what was to come, and knocked on the door. The sound echoed through the night, a hollow, reverberating noise that seemed to linger in the air long after it had faded.

For a moment, there was nothing but silence, and then, slowly, the door creaked open.

Aaron Blake stood in the doorway, his face shadowed, his expression unreadable.

"Detective Harris," Aaron said, his voice calm, almost resigned. "I've been expecting you."

Mark felt a shiver run down his spine as he met Aaron's gaze. The darkness that had gripped the town, the echoes, the deaths—it was all connected to this man, and the truth he was hiding.

And Mark knew that whatever happened next, there was no turning back.

Chapter 6: Shadows and Alliance

Aaron Blake sat in his office, staring at the dim light that filtered through the heavy curtains. The room, once a place of sterile order and clinical precision, now felt darker, more oppressive. The air was thick, carrying with it an unspoken tension that weighed on his chest like a stone. He had always kept the office meticulously organized, a sanctuary where he could maintain control over the chaos of his patients' minds. But now, as he sat behind his desk, he couldn't shake the feeling that the room was closing in on him.

The events of the past few days had shaken him to his core. The echoes that had haunted Elena Carter were no longer confined to her alone; they had begun to infiltrate his life as well, breaking through the walls he had so carefully constructed around his psyche. He had felt them, heard them, experienced them in ways that defied logic and reason. And yet, despite his training, despite his years of experience in the field of psychiatry, he couldn't explain what was happening.

Aaron's gaze drifted to the clock on the wall, its ticking unnervingly loud in the silence. It was almost time for his meeting with Detective Mark Harris, a man whose name had been mentioned by his assistant just a few hours earlier. The detective had requested a meeting, stating that he needed to discuss some urgent matters related to recent incidents in town. Aaron had agreed, though he wasn't entirely sure why. Perhaps it was the sense of unease that had been growing within him, the feeling that the events in Whistler's Grove were connected to the darkness that had begun to creep into his own life.

He had spent the last hour preparing for the meeting, going over his notes on Elena's case, trying to find a way to make sense of the inexplicable. But every time he thought he was close to an answer, the echoes would resurface, filling his mind with fragmented memories and emotions that weren't his own. It was as if the very act of searching for the truth only served to draw him deeper into the shadows.

A soft knock at the door pulled him from his thoughts, and Aaron straightened in his chair, his heart quickening. He took a deep breath, trying to steady himself before calling out, "Come in."

The door creaked open, and Mark Harris stepped into the room. The detective was tall and broad-shouldered, with a stern, weathered face that spoke of years spent dealing with the darker side of human nature. His eyes, sharp and penetrating, swept over the room before settling on Aaron. There was something in his gaze, a wariness, as if he were sizing Aaron up, trying to determine whether he could be trusted.

"Dr. Blake," Mark greeted him with a nod, his voice low and measured. "Thank you for agreeing to meet with me on such short notice."

Aaron stood and extended his hand, though he couldn't quite shake the sense of unease that lingered in the back of his mind. "Detective Harris, please have a seat. I understand you have some concerns you'd like to discuss."

Mark took the offered seat, his movements deliberate and controlled. He glanced around the room again, his eyes lingering on the shadows that seemed to pool in the corners. "This is a nice office you've got here," he said, though there was a hint of something in his tone—an edge that Aaron couldn't quite place.

"Thank you," Aaron replied, taking his seat behind the desk. He forced himself to maintain his composure, though he could feel the weight of the detective's scrutiny bearing down on him. "You mentioned that you wanted to discuss some recent incidents in town. How can I help?"

Mark leaned forward slightly, his elbows resting on his knees as he clasped his hands together. "I've been investigating a series of strange deaths in Whistler's Grove—deaths that, on the surface, don't seem connected. But I have reason to believe they might be."

Aaron frowned, his curiosity piqued. "Go on."

Mark reached into his jacket and pulled out a small notebook, flipping it open to a page filled with handwritten notes. "The victims were all found dead in their homes, with no signs of forced entry and no clear cause of death. What's more, each of them had been a patient at a psychiatric facility that was shut down years ago after a series of scandals. I've been looking into the records of that facility, and your name came up in connection with a few of the patients."

Aaron's heart skipped a beat, though he kept his expression neutral. He had been aware of the facility, of course—his father had worked there for a time, and Aaron had treated some of the former patients in the years since. But the connection between the deaths and the facility was news to him.

"I see," Aaron said slowly, his mind racing. "And you believe these deaths are somehow related to their time at the facility?"

Mark nodded, his gaze never leaving Aaron's face. "That's what I'm trying to figure out. The thing is, there's something... off about these cases. The victims were all found in a state of extreme fear, as if they died of fright. But there's no logical explanation for it. No signs of an intruder, no evidence of foul play. Just fear."

Aaron's fingers tightened around the edge of his desk, his thoughts flashing back to Elena's descriptions of the echoes, the way they had filled her with terror, with memories and emotions that weren't her own. Could it be possible that the echoes were somehow connected to these deaths? That the darkness that had begun to infiltrate his life was part of something much larger, something that had been set in motion years ago?

"Detective Harris," Aaron began carefully, choosing his words with precision, "what you're describing is highly unusual. In my experience, such extreme fear responses are often associated with psychological trauma—specifically, repressed memories or unresolved guilt. The mind has ways of protecting itself, of blocking out memories that are too painful to confront. But sometimes, those memories resurface, triggered by something in the environment, something that the patient may not even be aware of."

Mark listened intently, his expression thoughtful. "Are you saying these people were reliving some kind of trauma? Something from their time at the facility?"

"It's possible," Aaron replied, though he could feel the unease growing within him. "But what you're describing—dying of fear—it's not something I've encountered in my practice. Not in this way. There may be other factors at play here, factors that go beyond the psychological."

Mark's eyes narrowed slightly, as if he were trying to read between the lines of Aaron's words. "What kind of factors?"

Aaron hesitated, his mind racing. He knew that what he was about to suggest would sound absurd, even to someone as open-minded as Mark. But he couldn't shake the feeling that the echoes were connected to the deaths, that the darkness that had been unleashed was something beyond the realm of science.

"There are theories," Aaron said slowly, "about the nature of consciousness, about the way memories and emotions are stored in the mind. Some researchers believe that certain experiences, particularly traumatic ones, can leave an imprint on a person's psyche—a kind of echo that lingers long after the event itself has passed. In some cases, these echoes can be so strong that they take on a life of their own, influencing the person's behavior, their thoughts, even their physical health."

Mark's expression remained neutral, though Aaron could see the skepticism in his eyes. "You're talking about ghosts?"

"Not ghosts, exactly," Aaron replied, though he could feel his own skepticism wavering. "More like... remnants of past experiences.

Fragments of memory that have become detached from the person's conscious mind, but still exist somewhere in their subconscious. These echoes can be triggered by certain stimuli, causing the person to relive the experience as if it were happening in the present."

"And you think these echoes could be responsible for the deaths?" Mark asked, his tone cautious.

Aaron took a deep breath, his thoughts racing. He knew that what he was suggesting was highly unorthodox, even for someone in his field. But the more he considered it, the more it seemed to make sense. The victims had all been patients at the same facility, all had experienced trauma in one form or another. And now, years later, that trauma had resurfaced, triggered by something in their environment—something that had connected them to the darkness that had been unleashed.

"It's a possibility," Aaron said finally, though his voice was tinged with uncertainty. "But it's also possible that there's something else at work here, something that goes beyond the psychological. I've been working with a patient—Elena Carter—who has been experiencing something similar. She describes it as hearing echoes—voices, memories, emotions that aren't her own. And these echoes have been getting stronger, more intense, as if they're trying to take over."

Mark's eyes widened slightly at the mention of Elena's name, though he quickly masked his surprise. "Elena Carter? I've heard of her. She was involved in a car accident a few years ago, lost her sister, right?"

Aaron nodded, though he could feel the tension in the room growing. He hadn't expected Mark to be familiar with Elena's case, and the fact that he was only added to the sense of unease that had been building within him.

"Yes," Aaron replied, his voice cautious. "She was diagnosed with PTSD after the accident, but her symptoms have been... unusual. She describes them as echoes, and they seem to be getting stronger, more insistent. I've been trying to help her manage them, but it's becoming increasingly difficult."

Mark was silent for a moment, his gaze fixed on Aaron as if he were weighing his next words carefully. "You said these echoes can be triggered by something in the environment. Do you think that's what's happening here? That something in Whistler's Grove is triggering these echoes, causing people to relive their trauma?"

"It's possible," Aaron said, though he could feel the uncertainty in his own voice. "But I don't know what that trigger could be, or why it's happening now. There are too many unknowns, too many variables that I can't account for."

Mark leaned back in his chair, his expression thoughtful. "You said you've been trying to help Elena manage these echoes. How?"

Aaron hesitated, unsure of how much to reveal. He had always prided himself on his ability to maintain control, to keep his personal and professional lives separate. But the events of the past few days had blurred those lines, and he knew that he couldn't continue to ignore the connection between Elena's case and the deaths in Whistler's Grove.

"I've been using a combination of cognitive-behavioral therapy and mindfulness techniques," Aaron said finally, though he could feel the weight of his own words pressing down on him. "The idea is to help her identify and challenge the negative thought patterns that are associated with the echoes, to regain control over her mind. But it's becoming increasingly difficult. The echoes are growing stronger, more insistent, as if they're feeding off her fear."

Mark's expression remained neutral, though there was a flicker of something in his eyes—curiosity, perhaps, or concern. "And you think these techniques could help the others? The ones who've been affected by the echoes?"

"It's possible," Aaron replied, though he knew it was a weak answer. "But I don't know if it will be enough. The echoes seem to have a will of their own, a kind of malevolent intelligence that I don't fully understand. I've been researching supernatural folklore, trying to find some explanation for what's happening, but so far I've come up with nothing concrete."

Mark was silent for a moment, his gaze fixed on Aaron as if he were weighing his next move. "You're not just a psychiatrist, are you, Dr. Blake? You've got a personal stake in this, don't you?"

Aaron felt a chill run down his spine at Mark's words. He had always been careful to maintain a professional distance, to keep his emotions in check. But the events of the past few days had shaken him to his core, and he knew that he couldn't continue to pretend that this was just another case.

"Yes," Aaron admitted, his voice low. "I do have a personal stake in this. My father... he worked at the psychiatric facility where the victims were treated. He was involved in some experiments, experiments that went beyond the boundaries of science. And I believe that those experiments are connected to what's happening now."

Mark's eyes narrowed slightly, though he didn't seem surprised by the revelation. "What kind of experiments?"

"Memory manipulation," Aaron said, though the words felt heavy in his mouth. "My father was researching the nature of memory, specifically how traumatic experiences can fragment and distort it. He believed that by inducing dissociation, he could access repressed memories, memories that had been buried deep within the subconscious. But the experiments went wrong. The patients... they began to experience echoes, fragments of memory that took on a life of their own. And now, years later, those echoes have resurfaced, triggered by something in Whistler's Grove."

Mark was silent for a moment, his expression unreadable. "And you think these echoes are responsible for the deaths?"

"I don't know," Aaron admitted, though he could feel the weight of his own uncertainty pressing down on him. "But I believe that the echoes are connected to the darkness that's been unleashed. And if we don't find a way to stop it, more people will die."

Mark nodded slowly, his gaze fixed on Aaron as if he were trying to read the truth in his eyes. "Alright, Dr. Blake. We'll work together on this. But I need you to be straight with me. No more half-truths, no more holding back. If we're going to stop this, we need to be on the same page."

Aaron felt a flicker of relief at Mark's words, though the sense of unease still lingered. This was not a partnership born of trust or mutual respect—it was an alliance of necessity, forged in the face of a threat that neither of them fully understood.

"Agreed," Aaron said, though he knew that trust would be hard to come by. "I'll share everything I know, and I expect you to do the same."

Mark nodded, though there was still a wariness in his eyes. "Good. Now, where do we start?"

Aaron took a deep breath, his mind racing as he tried to piece together the fragments of information that had been swirling in his head. The echoes, the deaths, the darkness that had been unleashed—it was all connected, but the picture was still incomplete.

"We start with Elena," Aaron said finally, though the words felt heavy in his mouth. "She's the key. If we can understand what's happening to her, we might be able to find a way to stop it."

Mark nodded, his expression thoughtful. "Alright. But we'll need to move fast. I've got a feeling that whatever's happening, it's only going to get worse."

Aaron couldn't shake the feeling that Mark was right. The darkness was closing in, and they were running out of time.

As they stood to leave, Aaron couldn't shake the sense of foreboding that had settled over him. The uneasy alliance they had formed was a fragile one, built on a foundation of mutual suspicion and fear. But it was all they had, and they would need to rely on each other if they were to stand any chance of stopping the darkness that had begun to consume Whistler's Grove.

The shadows that lingered in the corners of the room seemed to deepen as they left the office, as if the darkness itself were watching, waiting for its moment to strike.

And Aaron knew, deep down, that the echoes were far from finished with them.

Chapter 7: Shadows of Doubt

The hospital's staff lounge was a stark contrast to the growing darkness in Aaron Blake's life. The room was bright and sterile, the white walls reflecting the harsh fluorescent lighting that buzzed softly overhead. It was a place designed for rest and respite, a haven where doctors and nurses could take a moment to catch their breath between shifts. But for Dr. Sarah Mitchell, the room felt cold, almost oppressive, as if the brightness only served to highlight the shadows lurking just out of sight.

Sarah sat at one of the small, round tables near the window, a cup of coffee in her hands. She stared out at the hospital courtyard below, watching as the late afternoon sun bathed the carefully manicured gardens in a warm, golden light. But the beauty of the scene did little to calm the unease that had been gnawing at her for days.

She had always prided herself on her ability to remain calm under pressure, to approach every challenge with a level head and a clear mind. But lately, something had been bothering her, something she couldn't quite put her finger on. And that something was Aaron Blake.

Aaron had always been a dedicated psychiatrist, methodical and precise in his approach to his work. But in recent weeks, Sarah had noticed a change in him—an obsession that had begun to consume him, drawing him deeper into a case that seemed to defy explanation. It wasn't just the intensity of his focus that concerned her; it was the way he had begun to withdraw, isolating himself from his colleagues, from her, as if he were hiding something.

Sarah took a sip of her coffee, her gaze still fixed on the courtyard below. She had tried to talk to Aaron, to express her concerns, but he had brushed her off, insisting that he was fine, that he was simply dealing with a challenging case. But Sarah knew Aaron too well. She could see the strain in his eyes, the way his hands trembled ever so slightly when he thought no one was looking. Something was wrong, and she was determined to find out what.

The door to the lounge opened, and Sarah glanced up to see Aaron step inside. He looked tired, his normally sharp features softened by exhaustion, dark circles under his eyes that spoke of sleepless nights. He paused when he saw her, a fleeting look of surprise crossing his face before he composed himself and crossed the room to where she sat.

"Sarah," Aaron greeted her with a faint smile, though it didn't reach his eyes. "I didn't expect to see you here. How have you been?"

Sarah set her coffee down, her eyes narrowing slightly as she studied him. "I've been fine, Aaron. But I'm more concerned about you. You've been... different lately."

Aaron's smile faltered, and he quickly looked away, feigning interest in the coffee pot on the counter. "I'm fine, Sarah. Just dealing with a particularly complex case. You know how it is."

Sarah didn't let him off the hook that easily. "Is it Elena Carter's case?"

Aaron stiffened at the mention of Elena's name, and that was all the confirmation Sarah needed. She leaned forward slightly, her voice softening. "Aaron, you've been spending a lot of time on that case. More than usual. I know you're dedicated, but... I'm worried about you. You're not yourself."

Aaron hesitated, his hand hovering over the coffee pot as he considered his next words. He finally sighed, pouring himself a cup of coffee before turning to face her. "Elena's case is... unique," he admitted, his tone cautious. "There are aspects to it that I've never encountered before. It's challenging, yes, but I'm handling it."

Sarah crossed her arms, leaning back in her chair as she regarded him with a mixture of concern and skepticism. "And what exactly makes it so unique? You've dealt with plenty of difficult cases before, Aaron. Why is this one different?"

Aaron's gaze flickered, a shadow passing over his face. "It's hard to explain," he said slowly, choosing his words with care. "Elena... she's experiencing something that goes beyond the usual symptoms of PTSD or dissociation. It's like she's tapping into something... something that I can't fully understand yet."

Sarah raised an eyebrow, her concern deepening. "Something you can't understand? Aaron, you're one of the most experienced psychiatrists I know. If you can't make sense of it, then maybe it's time to take a step back, to get a fresh perspective."

Aaron shook his head, his expression resolute. "I can't do that, Sarah. I need to see this through. I'm close to understanding what's happening to her, and I can't just walk away now."

Sarah bit her lip, her mind racing as she tried to make sense of what Aaron was telling her. He was clearly more invested in this case than he was letting on, and that only fueled her suspicion that there was more to the story than he was willing to share.

"Aaron," she said gently, her tone softening. "I know you're trying to help her, but you're also human. You can't carry the weight of this case alone. If you need help, if you need someone to talk to, I'm here."

Aaron met her gaze, and for a moment, Sarah saw the flicker of vulnerability in his eyes, the hint of the strain he was under. But then he quickly masked it, offering her another weak smile. "I appreciate that, Sarah. I really do. But I'm fine. I just need to focus on the work."

Sarah nodded slowly, though she wasn't convinced. "All right. But if you ever need to talk... you know where to find me."

Aaron nodded, taking a sip of his coffee before setting the cup down. "Thanks, Sarah. I'll keep that in mind."

But as he turned to leave, Sarah's mind was already racing, her concern for Aaron deepening with each passing moment. There was something he wasn't telling her, something that was eating away at him, and she couldn't just sit back and do nothing.

As Aaron left the lounge, Sarah stood up, her decision already made. She needed to find out more about Elena Carter, to understand why this case was affecting Aaron so deeply. And if Aaron wouldn't talk to her, then she would have to find the answers on her own.

Sarah finished her coffee and quickly made her way to her office, her mind already formulating a plan. She would start by reviewing Elena's file, looking for anything that might give her insight into the case. If there was something in Elena's past, something that connected her to the darkness that seemed to be consuming Aaron, Sarah would find it.

The hospital was quiet as she walked down the long, sterile hallways, the sound of her footsteps echoing off the polished floors. The late afternoon light filtered through the windows, casting long shadows that seemed to stretch endlessly down the corridors. But Sarah barely noticed, her focus entirely on the task ahead.

When she reached her office, Sarah quickly logged into the hospital's electronic medical records system, pulling up Elena Carter's file. As she scanned through the notes, her brow furrowed in concentration, searching for anything that might explain the strangeness of the case.

Elena's history was unremarkable at first glance—a childhood marked by loss and trauma, followed by a diagnosis of PTSD after a tragic car accident that had claimed the life of her younger sister. She had undergone therapy, medication, the usual treatment protocols for someone with her condition. But it was the more recent notes, the ones Aaron had made, that caught Sarah's attention.

The descriptions were unlike anything Sarah had encountered in her own practice. Aaron had noted the presence of "echoes," voices and visions that seemed to come from somewhere outside of Elena's own mind. The notes were detailed, meticulous, but they also hinted at something darker, something that Aaron himself was struggling to understand.

Sarah's heart raced as she read through the notes, her mind struggling to process the information. This wasn't just a case of PTSD or dissociation—there was something else at play here, something that defied the usual explanations. And whatever it was, it was affecting Aaron as well.

But what could it be? Sarah's thoughts turned to the possibility of a deeper, more insidious cause, something rooted in Elena's past. She needed to dig deeper, to uncover the connection between Elena's experiences and the darkness that seemed to be spreading through her life—and now, through Aaron's.

Sarah's fingers flew across the keyboard as she searched the hospital's archives, looking for any old case files that might be related to Elena's family or the psychiatric facility where she had been treated. It was a long shot, but Sarah had learned long ago that sometimes the most important clues were hidden in the past.

After what felt like hours of searching, Sarah finally found something—a file from the 1940s, long before Elena's time, but connected to the same psychiatric facility that had been shut down after the scandals. The file was incomplete, parts of it missing or redacted, but what remained was chilling.

The case involved a young woman named Margaret Carter, a patient at the facility who had been admitted after a series of violent outbursts. The notes described her as "hysterical" and "delusional," with visions and voices that seemed to torment her. But what caught Sarah's attention was the mention of "experimental treatments," procedures that were highly controversial even at the time.

Margaret had been subjected to a series of treatments that were intended to "cure" her of her delusions, but the notes hinted at something far more sinister. There were references to "memory manipulation" and "fragmentation," terms that were vague but ominous. And

then, suddenly, the notes stopped, the rest of the file missing or destroyed.

Sarah sat back in her chair, her mind racing. Could this Margaret Carter be a relative of Elena's? Was there some kind of family history, a legacy of trauma that had been passed down through the generations? And if so, what had happened to Margaret in that facility? What had they done to her?

The more Sarah thought about it, the more convinced she became that there was a connection. Elena's experiences, the echoes that haunted her—they seemed to mirror the symptoms described in Margaret's file. And if that was the case, then it was possible that whatever had been done to Margaret was now manifesting in Elena, passed down like a dark inheritance.

Sarah's heart pounded in her chest as she realized the implications. If this was true, then Aaron was dealing with something far more dangerous than a simple case of PTSD. He was dealing with the aftermath of unethical experiments, with a darkness that had been buried for decades, now resurfacing in the most terrifying way.

But what could she do? Sarah knew that she needed to confront Aaron, to share what she had found, but she also knew that he might not be receptive. He was too close to the case, too invested in finding answers on his own. And if he was already being affected by the echoes, then he might not be thinking clearly.

Sarah stood up, pacing the length of her office as she tried to figure out her next move. She couldn't just sit back and do nothing—Aaron needed to know what she had found, even if he didn't want to hear it. But how could she approach him without pushing him further away?

As she paced, Sarah's mind kept returning to the psychiatric facility, to the experiments that had been conducted there. There had to be more information, more records that could shed light on what had happened. But the files were sealed, locked away in bureaucratic limbo, and accessing them would be nearly impossible without the proper authorization.

Unless...

A thought occurred to Sarah, and she stopped in her tracks, her mind racing. There was one person who might be able to help, someone who had connections, who knew how to navigate the system. It was a long shot, but it was worth a try.

Sarah grabbed her phone, quickly dialing a number she hadn't called in years. As the phone rang, she felt a surge of anxiety, wondering if she was making the right decision. But before she could second-guess herself, the call was answered.

"Hello?"

"Dr. Langford?" Sarah's voice was steady, but her heart was racing. "It's Dr. Sarah Mitchell. I need your help."

There was a pause on the other end of the line, and then a deep, familiar voice responded. "Sarah? It's been a long time. What can I do for you?"

Sarah took a deep breath, quickly explaining the situation. Dr. Langford was a retired psychiatrist who had once been a mentor to her during her residency. He had connections in the medical community, particularly in the realm of historical records and archives. If anyone could help her access the sealed files, it was him.

As she finished explaining, Dr. Langford was silent for a moment, and Sarah held her breath, waiting for his response.

"That's a tall order, Sarah," he said finally, his tone thoughtful. "But I might be able to help. Give me some time, and I'll see what I can find."

Sarah exhaled, feeling a small sense of relief. "Thank you, Dr. Langford. I really appreciate it."

"Don't mention it," he replied. "Just be careful, Sarah. If what you're saying is true... this could be dangerous."

"I will," Sarah promised, though the warning only made her more determined. "I'll be in touch."

As she hung up the phone, Sarah felt a renewed sense of purpose. She wasn't sure what she would find, or if it would be enough to help Aaron, but she knew she had to try. The shadows were closing in, and she couldn't let Aaron face them alone.

But even as she steeled herself for the challenges ahead, Sarah couldn't shake the feeling that she was being drawn into something far bigger than she had anticipated. The echoes, the darkness—whatever was happening, it was more than just a case. It was a reckoning, one that had been building for decades, and now it was coming to a head.

And as Sarah prepared to confront Aaron with the truth, she knew that their lives would never be the same.

Chapter 8: The Echoes of Shadowbrook Asylum

The road leading to Shadowbrook Asylum was a narrow, winding path that cut through the dense woods on the outskirts of Whistler's Grove. The trees, gnarled and ancient, seemed to crowd the road, their branches interlocking overhead, casting the path in an oppressive, almost unnatural darkness. The sun was just beginning to set, and the fading light struggled to penetrate the thick canopy, casting long, eerie shadows that danced across the gravel as Aaron's car made its way up the road.

Aaron Blake gripped the steering wheel tightly, his knuckles white against the leather. Beside him, Elena Carter sat in tense silence, her eyes fixed on the road ahead, though it was clear her thoughts were far from the present. The silence between them was thick with unspoken fears, the air in the car heavy with the weight of what they were about to face.

The old asylum had been shut down decades ago, left to decay in the depths of the woods, its dark history forgotten by all but a few. But now, as they drew closer to its crumbling walls, the echoes of that past seemed to stir in the air, whispering of the horrors that had been buried within its walls.

Elena shifted in her seat, her hands clasped tightly in her lap. "Are you sure about this, Aaron?" Her voice was barely above a whisper, as if speaking too loudly might awaken something lurking in the shadows.

Aaron didn't take his eyes off the road, but he could feel the same unease gnawing at the edges of his mind. "We need answers, Elena. If we're going to understand what's happening to you—what's happening to us—we have to start at the source. And this place... this is where it all began."

Elena nodded, though her expression remained troubled. The echoes had been growing stronger, more vivid with each passing day, and the toll they were taking on her was becoming increasingly evident. Her once bright eyes were now shadowed with exhaustion, her skin pale and drawn. But there was a determination in her gaze that mirrored Aaron's own—a shared resolve to uncover the truth, no matter how terrifying it might be.

The car crested a small hill, and suddenly, the asylum came into view. Shadowbrook loomed ahead of them, its imposing structure half-hidden by the overgrown vegetation that had claimed the land around it. The building, once grand and austere, was now a ruin, its stone walls crumbling, its windows shattered and dark. Vines crawled up the sides of the building, their twisted tendrils wrapping around the columns and archways, as if trying to pull the asylum back into the earth.

Aaron parked the car at the edge of what had once been a driveway, now little more than a strip of cracked pavement barely visible beneath the encroaching weeds. The engine died with a soft hum, and for a moment, the only sound was the rustling of the leaves in the wind, a faint, mournful whisper that seemed to echo through the trees.

Elena shivered and pulled her coat tighter around her shoulders. "It's colder here," she murmured, her breath misting in the chill air. "Almost like the place itself is... dead."

Aaron glanced at her, his expression grim. "Maybe it is. Or maybe it's something worse."

They stepped out of the car, the ground crunching beneath their feet as they made their way toward the front entrance. The massive wooden doors were ajar, one hanging precariously on its hinges, the other leaning against the stone frame as if it had been ripped from its place long ago. The entrance hall beyond was shrouded in darkness, the faint light of the setting sun barely reaching the threshold.

Aaron hesitated at the door, a deep sense of foreboding settling in his chest. He had been in countless old buildings before—abandoned houses, forgotten churches—but none had ever felt like this. There was a presence here, something that lingered in the air like a thick fog, suffocating and inescapable.

He took a deep breath and stepped inside, his footsteps echoing off the cracked tiles. Elena followed closely behind, her hand brushing against the wall for support as they ventured deeper into the asylum.

The entrance hall was vast, the high ceiling supported by rows of columns that stretched into the shadows. Once, this place might have been grand, but now it was a hollow shell, stripped of all its former glory. The floor was littered with debris—fallen plaster, broken glass, and the remnants of old furniture, long since decayed. The walls were covered in peeling paint, revealing the cold stone beneath, and the air was thick with the scent of mold and damp.

Elena paused, her gaze drawn to the walls, where faint traces of old murals could still be seen. The paintings were faded and worn, but the images they depicted were disturbing—figures twisted in agony, faces contorted in fear, their eyes wide with terror. It was as if the walls themselves had absorbed the suffering of the people who had been confined within them, the pain and despair etched into the very fabric of the building.

Aaron noticed her staring and followed her gaze. His expression darkened as he recognized the scenes depicted in the murals—scenes of torment and madness, of minds broken by the horrors inflicted upon them. He had read about the experiments conducted at Shadowbrook, about the unethical practices that had taken place here in the name of science. But seeing it depicted so vividly, even in these faded images, brought a new level of horror to the reality of what had been done.

"This place... it's cursed," Elena whispered, her voice trembling. "I can feel it, Aaron. The echoes are stronger here... louder."

Aaron nodded, his own senses tingling with the energy that seemed to radiate from the very walls. "We need to find the records room," he said, his voice steady despite the fear gnawing at his insides. "If there are any files left, they might give us some insight into what happened here, into what your family—and mine—were involved in."

They continued deeper into the asylum, the darkness closing in around them as they ventured further from the entrance. The corridors were narrow, the walls lined with rusted metal doors, each one leading to a room that had once housed a patient. Most of the doors were ajar, their locks broken, revealing the small, barren cells within. The rooms were empty now, but the air was thick with the lingering presence of those who had once been trapped here, their voices echoing faintly in the back of Aaron's mind.

As they turned a corner, they came to a set of double doors, the word "Records" barely visible on the tarnished brass plaque that hung above them. Aaron pushed the doors open, and they creaked loudly, the sound echoing through the empty halls like a mournful wail.

The records room was large, the walls lined with rows of metal filing cabinets, each drawer labeled with the names of patients long forgotten. The air was musty, filled with the scent of old paper and dust, and the floor was covered in a thin layer of grime. A single window at the far end of the room let in a sliver of light, casting long shadows across the floor.

Elena hesitated at the threshold, her eyes wide as she took in the sight before her. "There must be thousands of files here," she murmured, her voice tinged with awe and dread. "How are we supposed to find anything?"

Aaron stepped inside, his gaze scanning the room. "We'll start with the files that are most likely to be relevant. Look for any names you recognize—Carter, Blake, anyone connected to your family or mine. We don't have much time before it gets too dark to see anything."

Elena nodded and moved to the nearest filing cabinet, her hands trembling slightly as she pulled open one of the drawers. The metal groaned in protest, but it yielded, revealing a stack of yellowed files, each one tied with a piece of frayed string. She picked up the first file, her fingers brushing against the brittle paper, and began to read.

Aaron did the same, moving to a cabinet on the opposite side of the room. He flipped through the files quickly, scanning the names and dates, searching for anything that might shed light on the dark history of Shadowbrook.

As the minutes ticked by, the room grew quieter, the only sound the rustling of papers and the occasional creak of the building settling around them. The air seemed to grow heavier, the shadows deepening as the light outside faded, and with it came a sense of urgency, as if time itself were running out.

It was Elena who found the first clue—a file labeled "Margaret Carter." Her heart skipped a beat as she opened it, her eyes quickly scanning the contents. The file detailed Margaret's treatment at the asylum, her struggles with dissociative episodes and auditory hallucinations. But there was something more, something that caught Elena's attention—a note written in the margins, in a different hand than the rest of the file.

"Experiment No. 47 – Subject displays heightened sensitivity to echoes. Further observation required."

Elena's breath caught in her throat as she read the words. She had heard the term "echoes" before, but only in the context of her own experiences. The idea that her ancestor had also been sensitive to these echoes, that she had been part of some kind of experiment—it was almost too much to comprehend.

"Aaron," she called, her voice tight with emotion. "You need to see this."

Aaron crossed the room quickly, taking the file from her hands. His eyes scanned the document, his expression growing darker with each passing moment. "This is it," he muttered, more

to himself than to Elena. "This is the connection we've been looking for."

He handed the file back to her, his mind already racing ahead to the implications of what they had found. "There must be more," he said, turning back to the cabinets. "If your ancestor was part of these experiments, then there's a good chance others were too. We need to find out who else was involved."

Elena nodded, her hands shaking slightly as she continued to sift through the files. The knowledge that her own bloodline was tied to the dark history of this place was both terrifying and strangely validating. She wasn't crazy—there was a reason for what she was experiencing, a reason rooted in the past.

They worked in silence, the air around them growing colder as the last light of day faded, leaving them in near darkness. Aaron had just pulled out another file when he felt it—a sudden, intense pressure in his chest, as if the air had been sucked out of the room. He gasped, dropping the file as he stumbled back, his hand clutching at his chest.

Elena looked up, alarmed. "Aaron, what's wrong?"

But Aaron couldn't answer. His vision blurred, and suddenly, the room around him seemed to shift, the walls melting away as he was plunged into a memory that wasn't his own.

He was standing in a room, the walls lined with shelves filled with jars and vials, each one labeled with strange symbols. The air was thick with the scent of chemicals, and the only light came from a single, flickering bulb overhead. In the center of the room was a table, and on that table lay a figure, strapped down, their face obscured by a metal mask.

Aaron's heart raced as he recognized the scene—it was a laboratory, one of the places where the experiments had been conducted. He could feel the fear, the pain radiating from the figure on the table, their body trembling as they struggled against the restraints.

And then, he heard it—a voice, low and malevolent, speaking in a language he didn't understand. The words were like poison, seeping into his mind, twisting his thoughts, filling him with a darkness that was all-consuming.

The voice grew louder, more insistent, and with it came the echoes—waves of memories, not his own, crashing over him, pulling him under. He saw flashes of faces, heard screams, felt the terror of those who had been subjected to the experiments, their minds shattered, their souls broken.

Aaron fell to his knees, his hands clutching at his head as he tried to block out the voices, the images. But they wouldn't stop—they were relentless, clawing at him, dragging him deeper into the darkness.

And then, just as suddenly as it had begun, it stopped. The voices, the images, the pain—it all faded, leaving Aaron gasping for breath on the cold, dirty floor of the records room.

Elena was at his side, her face pale with fear. "Aaron, what happened? What did you see?"

Aaron took a shaky breath, his hands trembling as he tried to steady himself. "I saw... I saw one of the experiments. They were... they were trying to harness the echoes, to control them. But it went wrong... so wrong."

Elena's eyes widened, her own fear reflected in his. "Aaron, we need to leave. This place... it's not safe."

But Aaron shook his head, his determination hardening. "Not yet. There's something here—something we need to find. We're so close, Elena. We can't stop now."

Elena looked torn, but she nodded, knowing that Aaron was right. Whatever was happening to them, whatever darkness they were uncovering, they needed to see it through to the end.

They continued searching the room, their movements hurried now, driven by the sense that time was running out. Aaron could feel the echoes pressing in on him, could hear the faint whispers growing louder with each passing moment. But he pushed it aside, focusing on the task at hand.

And then, finally, they found it—a small, leather-bound journal, hidden at the back of one of the drawers. The cover was worn, the pages yellowed with age, but the writing inside was still legible.

Aaron opened the journal, his eyes scanning the first few pages. It was written in his father's hand, the familiar script both comforting and chilling. The entries detailed the experiments, the notes growing more erratic as the journal progressed, the handwriting becoming more frantic, more desperate.

"They were trying to open a doorway," Aaron murmured, his voice trembling with the realization. "They believed the echoes were a gateway to another realm, a place where they could tap into a power beyond anything they could imagine. But they didn't understand... they didn't realize what they were unleashing."

Elena's breath caught in her throat as she looked over Aaron's shoulder, reading the words for herself. "A doorway... to where?"

Aaron shook his head, his mind racing. "I don't know. But whatever it is, it's here. It's been here all along, trapped in this place, feeding off the echoes, growing stronger."

The room seemed to close in around them, the air thick with the weight of the revelation. They had uncovered the truth, but in doing so, they had awakened something dark, something that had been lying dormant for decades, waiting for the right moment to strike.

Aaron closed the journal, his expression grim. "We need to get out of here. Now."

But as they turned to leave, the room suddenly went cold, the temperature dropping so rapidly that their breath fogged the air. The shadows seemed to lengthen, stretching out from the corners of the room, reaching for them with unseen hands.

Elena gasped, her eyes wide with terror. "Aaron... what's happening?"

Aaron didn't answer. He knew what was happening—the echoes, the darkness, the malevolent force they had uncovered—it was all coming for them. The asylum was no longer just a building; it was a living entity, a place where the lines between the physical and the supernatural had been blurred, where the past and the present had become one.

And now, they were trapped inside it.

"Run," Aaron whispered, grabbing Elena's hand and pulling her toward the door. "Run!"

They sprinted down the hallway, their footsteps echoing off the walls as the shadows chased them, the air filled with the sound of whispers and distant screams. The asylum seemed to twist around them, the corridors stretching out into infinity, the exits disappearing before their eyes.

But Aaron didn't stop. He couldn't stop. He had to get Elena out of here, had to escape the darkness that was closing in on them.

Finally, they reached the entrance hall, the massive doors looming ahead of them like a beacon of hope. Aaron didn't slow down, throwing his weight against the door as they burst outside, the cold night air hitting them like a wave of relief.

They stumbled to a stop, gasping for breath as they turned back to the asylum. The building stood silent and still, the shadows retreating into the darkness as if nothing had happened.

But something had happened—something that had changed them both forever.

Elena clung to Aaron, her body trembling with fear. "What was that, Aaron? What did we awaken?"

Aaron shook his head, his mind still reeling from the experience. "I don't know. But whatever it is, it's not done with us yet."

They stood there for a long moment, staring at the dark, silent asylum, knowing that they had only just begun to uncover the horrors that lay within its walls.

The past had come alive, and the echoes of Shadowbrook were only just beginning to make themselves heard.

Chapter 9: The Dark Tapestry

Detective Mark Harris sat in his office, the dim light from the desk lamp casting long shadows across the room. The walls were covered with crime scene photos, maps, and newspaper clippings, all connected by lines of red string that crisscrossed the room like a web of blood. The faces of the victims stared back at him from the walls, their expressions frozen in terror, their deaths an unsolved mystery that gnawed at his conscience.

Mark leaned back in his chair, rubbing his temples as he tried to make sense of the mounting evidence. His desk was littered with reports, autopsy photos, and handwritten notes—each one a piece of a puzzle that refused to come together. The air in the room was thick with the scent of stale coffee and cigarette smoke, a reminder of the long hours he had spent pouring over the details, trying to find the thread that would unravel the truth.

But the more he looked, the more elusive the truth became.

Mark's eyes were drawn to the map on the wall, where he had marked the locations of each crime with a small red pin. The points formed a rough circle around the outskirts of Whistler's Grove, with Shadowbrook Asylum at the center. It was as if the town itself was a trap, the victims drawn into a web of darkness that radiated out from the old, abandoned asylum.

He stared at the map, his mind racing. The pattern was clear, but the meaning was not. How were these deaths connected to the asylum? What was the link that tied them all together?

Mark reached for the file on the latest victim, John Wilkes, and flipped it open. The man had been found dead in his home, his body contorted in fear, with no signs of a struggle. The autopsy report had been inconclusive—no drugs, no toxins, no physical trauma. Just a heart that had stopped, as if the man had been scared to death.

But what had scared him? What had driven him to that point?

Mark's gaze shifted to the photograph of John Wilkes' body, his face twisted in terror, his eyes wide open as if he had seen something too horrifying to comprehend. Mark had seen that expression before, in the other victims, in the photos that now lined the walls of his office.

He pushed the file aside and reached for another, his mind drifting back to the conversations he had had with Aaron Blake. The psychiatrist had spoken of echoes, of memories that weren't their own, of a force that was beyond their understanding. Mark had dismissed it at first, chalking it up to the stress of the investigation, but now he wasn't so sure.

The more he delved into the history of Whistler's Grove, the more he realized that there was something dark buried in the town's past—something that was resurfacing, claiming victims one by one.

Mark stood up and began pacing the room, his mind racing as he tried to piece together the fragments of information. The town's history was long and twisted, filled with stories of unexplained deaths, mysterious disappearances, and rumors of curses. But there was one thread that kept appearing, one place that seemed to be at the center of it all—Shadowbrook Asylum.

The asylum had been built in the late 1800s, during a time when mental illness was poorly understood and even more poorly treated. It had been a place of experimentation, where doctors had pushed the boundaries of medical ethics in their quest to cure the incurable. But those experiments had gone wrong—terribly wrong. Patients had died, and the asylum had been shut down, its dark history buried beneath layers of secrecy and shame.

But the past had a way of resurfacing, and now it seemed that whatever had been unleashed in that place was coming back to haunt the town.

Mark stopped in front of the map, his eyes narrowing as he traced the lines of red string with his finger. The pattern was clear—the victims were all connected to the asylum, either directly or through their families. But there was more to it than that. There was a darkness that had taken root in the town, something that had been festering for decades, waiting for the right moment to strike.

He reached for a notebook on his desk and flipped to a page where he had jotted down notes on the town's history. The stories he had uncovered were chilling—tales of cursed lands, of vengeful spirits, of dark rituals performed in the dead of night. Some of the oldest stories spoke of a land that was tainted, a place where the veil between the living and the dead was thin, where the spirits of the dead could cross over and take their revenge.

Mark had always been a skeptic, a man of logic and reason. But as he delved deeper into the history of Whistler's Grove, he couldn't shake the feeling that there was something more at play here—something that went beyond the physical world, something that was rooted in the very land itself.

He sat back down at his desk and began flipping through the notes he had taken on various cultural beliefs in the afterlife. Different cultures had different ways of explaining the unexplainable, different ways of dealing with death and what came after. But there was a common thread that ran through many of these beliefs—the idea that the dead could influence the living, that they could return to seek justice, or revenge, or simply to be remembered.

In some cultures, the dead were believed to linger in the places where they had suffered the most, their spirits trapped by the trauma they had experienced. These places were often considered cursed, places where the living would do well to tread lightly, lest they awaken the spirits that lay dormant there.

Mark had dismissed such stories as superstition, the product of primitive minds trying to make sense of a world they didn't understand. But now, as he stared at the map of Whistler's Grove, he began to wonder if there wasn't some truth to them after all.

The victims weren't just random people—they were all connected to the asylum, either through their own experiences or through their families. And the asylum itself was built on land that had long been considered cursed, a place where the boundary between the living and the dead was thin, where the echoes of the past could still be heard.

Mark's mind raced as he tried to piece together the puzzle. The asylum had been built on cursed land, and the experiments conducted there had only served to amplify the darkness that was already present. The patients who had suffered and died in that place hadn't just been victims of cruel and unethical practices—they had been victims of something far darker, something that had been unleashed by those experiments.

And now, decades later, that darkness was still there, waiting for the right moment to strike.

Mark stood up and began pacing the room again, his mind racing. He had always believed that there was a logical explanation for everything, that every crime could be solved if you just found the right evidence. But this... this was something else entirely. This wasn't just a series of murders—this was something deeper, something that went beyond the physical world.

He stopped in front of the map again, his eyes narrowing as he studied the red pins that marked the locations of the crimes. The pattern was clear—the victims were all connected to the asylum, and the crimes were all centered around that place. But what was the connection? What was it that had been unleashed in that place, and how was it still affecting the town all these years later?

Mark's mind drifted back to the conversation he had had with Aaron Blake. The psychiatrist had spoken of echoes, of memories that weren't their own, of a force that was beyond their understanding. Mark had dismissed it at first, but now he began to wonder if Aaron wasn't on to something.

What if the echoes were more than just memories? What if they were a manifestation of the darkness that had been unleashed in that place, a darkness that was now spreading through the town, claiming victims one by one?

Mark sat back down at his desk and began flipping through the files again, his mind racing. The victims were all connected to the asylum, and the crimes were all centered around that place. But there was more to it than that. There was a darkness that had taken root in the town, something that had been festering for decades, waiting for the right moment to strike.

He picked up the file on Margaret Carter, one of the earliest victims, and began reading through it again. Margaret had been a patient at the asylum, admitted for what the doctors had described as severe dissociative episodes and auditory hallucinations. But there was something more, something that caught Mark's attention—a note written in the margins of the file, in a different hand than the rest of the document.

"Subject displays heightened sensitivity to echoes. Further observation required."

Mark's heart skipped a beat as he read the words. The term "echoes" had come up before, in his conversations with Aaron, but now he was seeing it in the official records of the asylum. This wasn't just a figment of Aaron's imagination—this was something real, something that the doctors at the asylum had been aware of, and had even tried to study.

He flipped through the rest of the file, his eyes scanning the pages for more clues. The notes were sparse, but there was enough to piece together a rough picture of what had happened. Margaret had been subjected to a series of experiments, designed to test her sensitivity to these echoes. The doctors had believed that by harnessing this sensitivity, they could tap into a power beyond anything they could imagine—a power that would allow them to control the minds of others, to manipulate reality itself.

But the experiments had gone wrong. Margaret's condition had deteriorated rapidly, and she had begun to experience terrifying visions, seeing things that weren't there, hearing voices that no one else could hear. The doctors had tried to treat her with sed

atives and electroshock therapy, but nothing had worked. In the end, Margaret had died under mysterious circumstances—her death officially recorded as a suicide, though the details were vague.

Mark sat back in his chair, his mind reeling. The asylum hadn't just been a place of experimentation—it had been a place where the boundaries between the living and the dead had been blurred, where the echoes of the past had been brought to life, with devastating consequences.

And now, those echoes were still there, still waiting, still hungry.

Mark's thoughts were interrupted by a knock at the door. He looked up to see Officer Claire Benson standing in the doorway, her expression serious.

"Detective Harris," she said, stepping into the room. "We've got another one."

Mark's heart sank. Another victim. Another life claimed by the darkness that was spreading through the town.

"Where?" he asked, already reaching for his coat.

"Edge of town, near the old mill," Claire replied. "Same MO as the others—no signs of forced entry, no obvious cause of death. Just... dead."

Mark nodded, his mind already racing ahead. The old mill was near the asylum, another point on the map, another victim drawn into the web of darkness that radiated out from that place.

"Let's go," he said, his voice tight with determination. "We need to stop this before it's too late."

As they made their way out of the office, Mark couldn't shake the feeling that time was running out. The darkness was closing in, the echoes growing stronger with each passing day. And if they didn't find a way to stop it, to contain the darkness, it would consume them all.

As they drove through the quiet streets of Whistler's Grove, Mark's mind raced. The victims were all connected to the asylum, and the crimes were all centered around that place. But there was more to it than that. There was a darkness that had taken root in the town, something that had been festering for decades, waiting for the right moment to strike.

And now, that moment had come.

Mark's thoughts drifted back to the conversation he had had with Aaron Blake. The psychiatrist had spoken of echoes, of memories that weren't their own, of a force that was beyond their understanding. Mark had dismissed it at first, but now he began to wonder if Aaron wasn't on to something.

What if the echoes were more than just memories? What if they were a manifestation of the darkness that had been unleashed in that place, a darkness that was now spreading through the town, claiming victims one by one?

Mark clenched his fists, his resolve hardening. He didn't know what they were dealing with, didn't know how to stop it. But he knew one thing for sure—he wouldn't rest until he had found a way to put an end to the darkness that was threatening to consume the town.

As they arrived at the crime scene, Mark's gaze was drawn to the old mill in the distance, its silhouette looming against the darkening sky. The building was a relic of the town's past, abandoned and forgotten, much like the asylum. But now, it seemed to pulse with a malevolent energy, a reminder of the darkness that lay hidden in the town's history.

Mark stepped out of the car, his breath misting in the cold air. The scene was eerily quiet, the only sound the crunch of gravel underfoot as he and Claire approached the house. The front door was ajar, and Mark could feel the weight of the darkness pressing down on him as he stepped inside.

The interior was just as he had expected—dim, cold, and filled with the stench of decay. The furniture was overturned, the walls marked with scratches, as if the victim had been trying to claw their way out. And there, in the center of the room, was the body—slumped in a chair, the face twisted in terror, the eyes wide open, staring at something only they could see.

Mark crouched down next to the body, his mind racing as he took in the scene. There were no signs of a struggle, no signs of forced entry. Just like the other victims, it was as if the man had been scared to death.

But scared of what?

Mark's gaze shifted to the walls, where faint traces of old wallpaper could still be seen, the pattern barely visible beneath the layers of grime. But there was something else—something that caught his attention. Symbols, scratched into the walls, almost hidden beneath the peeling paper.

He reached out and traced one of the symbols with his finger, his mind flashing back to the notes he had taken on occult practices. The symbol was old, ancient even, and it was one he had seen before—in the files on the asylum.

Mark stood up, his heart pounding in his chest. The symbols, the echoes, the darkness—they were all connected, all part of a larger tapestry that was only now beginning to reveal itself.

He turned to Claire, his expression grim. "We need to talk to Aaron Blake. Now."

As they made their way back to the car, Mark couldn't shake the feeling that they were on the brink of something terrible, something that had been building for decades. The darkness was spreading, the echoes growing louder, and if they didn't find a way to stop it, the town of Whistler's Grove would be consumed by the shadows that had been lurking just beneath the surface for so long.

The past was catching up with them, and the echoes of old sins were beginning to make themselves heard.

Chapter 10: The Shadows Within

The air inside Aaron Blake's home was heavy, almost suffocating, as if the walls themselves were closing in on him. It had once been a place of refuge, a sanctuary where he could escape the chaos of the world and find solace in his solitude. But now, the house felt oppressive, the darkness seeping into every corner, tainting the familiar spaces with an unshakable sense of dread.

Aaron sat in the dim light of his living room, the silence around him thick and unnatural. He could feel it—an unseen presence lurking just beyond the edges of his perception, watching, waiting. His heart pounded in his chest, a steady drumbeat of fear that he couldn't ignore, no matter how much he tried to convince himself that it was all in his head.

But deep down, he knew better. The events of the past few days had shattered his carefully constructed world of logic and reason. The echoes, the visions, the darkness that seemed to follow him wherever he went—they were all too real, too vivid to be dismissed as mere hallucinations.

His gaze drifted to the old journal sitting on the coffee table, its leather cover worn and cracked with age. It was his father's journal, the one he had found in the depths of Shadowbrook Asylum. The journal that had revealed the terrible truth about the experiments conducted there, about the malevolent force that had been unleashed.

The force that was now coming for him.

Aaron leaned back in his chair, his thoughts racing. He had spent years trying to bury the memories of his mother's breakdown, of the night she had been taken away. But now, those memories were resurfacing, dragging him back into the darkness he had tried so hard to escape.

He closed his eyes, trying to calm his racing thoughts, but the silence was soon filled with the sound of his mother's voice—a voice that he hadn't heard in years, but one that had haunted his dreams ever since.

"Aaron... Aaron, where are you?"

Her voice was soft, almost a whisper, but it was enough to send a chill down his spine. He opened his eyes, his heart skipping a beat as he saw her standing in the doorway, her figure bathed in the soft glow of the moonlight filtering through the window.

She looked just as he remembered her—beautiful, with long dark hair that framed her delicate features. But there was something wrong, something off. Her eyes were too wide, too bright, and there was a hollow, almost desperate edge to her smile.

"Aaron," she whispered again, stepping closer. "Why didn't you come to me? Why did you leave me alone?"

Aaron's breath caught in his throat, his mind struggling to comprehend what he was seeing. This wasn't real—it couldn't be. His mother had been dead for years, lost to the darkness that had consumed her mind.

But the figure before him was so real, so vivid, that he couldn't help but doubt his own senses. He stood up slowly, his legs trembling as he took a step toward her.

"Mom?" His voice was barely a whisper, thick with emotion. "How... how are you here?"

She smiled, but it was a smile devoid of warmth, a hollow expression that sent a wave of fear crashing over him. "You left me, Aaron. You abandoned me when I needed you most. And now... now you're going to pay."

Her voice twisted, growing deeper, more sinister, as her face contorted into a mask of rage. The light in the room dimmed, the shadows lengthening, creeping toward him like living entities.

Aaron stumbled back, his mind reeling as the walls around him seemed to close in. This wasn't his mother—it was something else, something dark and malevolent, using her image to torment him.

The room shifted, the furniture warping and twisting as if the house itself were alive, reacting to the force that had taken hold. The air grew thick with the scent of decay, a sickly sweet odor that made Aaron gag.

"Mom, please," he begged, his voice breaking. "I'm sorry... I'm so sorry..."

But the figure before him only laughed, a cold, cruel sound that echoed through the room. "Sorry won't bring me back, Aaron. Sorry won't undo what you did."

The walls began to tremble, the pictures on the walls falling to the floor with a crash. The lights flickered, casting eerie shadows that danced across the walls, twisting into grotesque shapes.

Aaron's heart raced, his mind spiraling into panic as he backed away from the figure that had once been his mother. The memories of that night came flooding back, memories he had tried so hard to bury—his mother's screams, the sound of breaking glass, the sight of her being dragged away by the paramedics as she begged him to help her.

He had been just a boy, powerless to stop what was happening, powerless to save her. And now, the guilt that he had carried with him all these years was being used against him, twisted by the malevolent force that had taken hold of his mind.

"Aaron!" The voice was Elena's, cutting through the darkness like a beacon of light.

He turned toward the sound, his vision blurring as the room continued to twist and warp around him. Elena was there, standing in the doorway, her face pale with fear.

"Get away from her!" she shouted, rushing toward him.

But the figure that had taken the form of his mother only laughed, a deep, guttural sound that sent a shiver down Aaron's spine. "She can't save you, Aaron. No one can save you now."

The walls began to close in, the shadows growing thicker, darker, as if the very essence of the house was being consumed by the malevolent force. The figure before him twisted, her face warping into something monstrous, something inhuman.

"Aaron, look at me!" Elena's voice was desperate, her hands gripping his shoulders, shaking him as if trying to pull him out of the nightmare that had taken hold.

But Aaron couldn't tear his eyes away from the figure before him, the image of his mother that had been twisted into something grotesque, something evil. The memories of that night played out in his mind, over and over, each time more vivid, more painful, until he could no longer distinguish between past and present.

"Aaron, please," Elena whispered, her voice breaking. "You have to fight it. This isn't real... it's not her."

But the force that had taken hold of him was too strong, too deeply rooted in the guilt and trauma that had haunted him for years. He could feel it burrowing into his mind, feeding on his fear, his pain, twisting his memories into something dark and malevolent.

Elena's grip tightened, her voice trembling with emotion. "Aaron, I need you to come back to me. I need you to fight this."

But Aaron was lost, trapped in the nightmare that had been unleashed upon him. The figure before him—the twisted image of his mother—reached out, her fingers brushing against his cheek.

"You're mine now, Aaron," she whispered, her voice a chilling echo that reverberated through his mind. "You'll never escape me."

The darkness closed in, the walls of the room seeming to collapse in on themselves, the shadows swallowing everything in their path. Aaron could feel his mind unraveling, the force that had taken hold of him dragging him deeper into the abyss.

But then, through the darkness, he felt a spark—a tiny flicker of light that cut through the shadows, reaching for him, pulling him back.

It was Elena. Her voice, her presence, was the only thing tethering him to reality, the only thing keeping him from being completely consumed by the darkness.

"Fight it, Aaron," she pleaded, her voice filled with desperation. "Please, don't let it take you."

Her words were like a lifeline, a thread of hope that he clung to with all his strength. He focused on her voice, on the warmth of her hands on his shoulders, on the light that seemed to emanate from her, pushing back the shadows that threatened to engulf him.

The force that had taken hold of him screamed in rage, its grip on his mind tightening as it tried to drag him back into the darkness. But Aaron fought back, drawing on every ounce of strength he had left, refusing to let the malevolent force win.

With a final surge of willpower, he broke free, the darkness receding as he was pulled back into the light. The figure of his mother dissolved into smoke, the oppressive atmosphere of the room lifting as the shadows retreated.

Aaron collapsed to the floor, gasping for breath, his body trembling with exhaustion. Elena was at his side in an instant, her arms wrapping around him, holding him close as he fought to steady his breathing.

"It's okay," she whispered, her voice soothing. "You're okay now."

But Aaron knew better. He wasn't okay—none of this was okay. The force that had attacked him was growing stronger, feeding on his guilt, his trauma, using his own mind against him. And it wasn't going to stop—not until it had consumed everything.

He pulled away from Elena, his eyes wide with fear. "It's not over," he said, his voice hoarse. "It's getting stronger, Elena. It's feeding on me, on my memories, my guilt. And if we don't find a way to stop it…"

He didn't need to finish the sentence. The look in Elena's eyes told him that she understood all too well.

"We will stop it," she said firmly, her voice filled with a determination that belied the fear in her eyes. "We'll find a way, Aaron. We have to."

But even as

she spoke the words, Aaron could see the doubt in her eyes, the fear that they were both too late. The force that had been unleashed was ancient, powerful, and it was rooted in the very fabric of the town, in the land itself.

He glanced around the room, at the remnants of the attack—the shattered glass, the fallen pictures, the lingering sense of unease that clung to the walls like a dark cloud. This house, his home, had become a battleground, a place where the past and the present were colliding in the most terrifying way possible.

And he knew, with a sinking feeling in his gut, that it was only going to get worse.

Elena stood up, her hand outstretched to help him to his feet. "We need to get out of here," she said quietly. "This place… it's not safe anymore."

Aaron nodded, his mind still reeling from the experience. He took her hand, allowing her to pull him to his feet, his legs unsteady beneath him. The house seemed to shift around them, the walls creaking as if protesting their presence.

They made their way to the front door, the oppressive atmosphere lifting slightly as they stepped outside into the cool night air. The sky was clear, the stars twinkling above them like distant beacons of hope, but the darkness that clung to Aaron's mind refused to dissipate.

He turned to look back at the house, the familiar structure now seeming like a stranger, a place that no longer offered safety or comfort. The shadows that lurked within its walls were too deep, too dark, and he knew that as long as they stayed here, they would never be free of the force that was hunting them.

Elena's voice broke through his thoughts, soft and filled with concern. "Aaron... what happened in there? What did you see?"

He hesitated, his gaze still fixed on the house. "It wasn't just a memory," he said slowly, his voice barely above a whisper. "It was... something more. Something that used my mother's image to get to me, to break me."

Elena's hand tightened on his arm, her fear palpable. "The force... it's stronger than we thought. It's not just feeding on your guilt—it's using it against you."

Aaron nodded, the weight of her words settling heavily on his shoulders. "And it's not just me, Elena. It's everyone who's been touched by this place, by what happened at Shadowbrook. The echoes... they're not just memories. They're alive, and they're growing stronger with each passing day."

Elena shivered, the night air suddenly feeling much colder. "We have to find a way to stop it, Aaron. Before it's too late."

He turned to face her, his eyes filled with a determination that belied the fear that still lingered in his heart. "We will. But we can't do it alone. We need help—someone who understands what we're dealing with, who knows how to fight it."

Elena nodded, her resolve hardening. "Then we find that help, Aaron. Whatever it takes, we find a way to stop this before it consumes us all."

As they stood there, side by side in the darkness, the weight of their task pressed down on them like a heavy shroud. The force that had been unleashed was ancient, powerful, and it was rooted in their very souls.

But they knew that they couldn't run from it, couldn't hide from the darkness that was closing in around them.

They had to face it, confront the shadows within themselves, and find a way to banish the malevolent force that was threatening to consume them all.

And as they walked away from the house, leaving the echoes of the past behind, they knew that their fight was only just beginning.

Chapter 11: The Awakening

Sarah Mitchell's home was a sanctuary, a place where order and calm reigned supreme. Every item had its place, every surface was meticulously clean, and the air carried a faint scent of lavender, her favorite essential oil. The walls were adorned with framed photographs of serene landscapes, and the soft lighting created an atmosphere of warmth and tranquility. It was a space that reflected Sarah's personality—organized, controlled, and above all, safe.

But as she sat in her living room that evening, her mind was far from the peace that her surroundings offered. The events of the past few days had shaken her, left her questioning things she had always taken for granted. Aaron's obsession with Elena Carter's case, the dark history of Shadowbrook Asylum, and the strange, unsettling incidents that had been happening in Whistler's Grove—everything seemed to be spiraling out of control, and for someone like Sarah, who thrived on order, it was deeply unsettling.

She had tried to push the thoughts aside, to focus on the tasks at hand, but they kept creeping back into her mind, gnawing at her, refusing to be ignored. There was a darkness lurking just beneath the surface of everything, a darkness that she couldn't quite explain but that she felt with every fiber of her being.

Sarah stood up from the couch, the soft fabric of her robe brushing against her skin as she walked to the kitchen. She needed to distract herself, to do something that would bring her back to the calm, controlled world she had created for herself. She reached for the kettle, filling it with water and setting it on the stove, the familiar routine of making tea providing a small measure of comfort.

As she waited for the water to boil, Sarah's thoughts drifted back to the file she had found in the archives, the one that had linked Elena Carter to Margaret Carter, a former patient at the asylum. The connection between the two women had been undeniable, and it had shaken Sarah to her core. She had always believed in science, in facts and evidence, but the more she learned about this case, the more she began to doubt everything she had once held dear.

Her mind wandered to the conversation she had had with Aaron earlier that day. He had spoken of echoes, of memories that weren't their own, of a force that was beyond their understanding. At the time, she had dismissed it as stress, the result of too many sleepless nights and too much emotional turmoil. But now, as she stood alone in her quiet kitchen, she couldn't shake the feeling that there was something more to it, something that went beyond the physical world.

The kettle whistled, and Sarah poured the hot water over the tea bag, watching as the dark liquid seeped into the cup. The simple act of making tea should have been grounding, a return to normalcy, but instead, it only heightened her sense of unease. The silence in the house felt oppressive, the shadows in the corners of the room seemed to shift and move in ways they hadn't before.

Sarah took the cup of tea and walked back to the living room, settling into her favorite armchair by the window. The night outside was calm, the moon casting a soft glow over the quiet street. But the tranquility of the scene did nothing to quell the storm brewing inside her.

She sipped her tea, the warmth spreading through her, but it didn't chase away the cold knot of anxiety that had taken up residence in her chest. Her thoughts turned to the patient she had lost years ago—the one whose death had haunted her ever since. She had been young, fresh out of residency, and full of hope that she could make a difference in the world. But she had failed, and the guilt of that failure had stayed with her, a shadow that followed her no matter how much she tried to outrun it.

As she sat there, the cup of tea growing cold in her hands, Sarah felt a strange sensation wash over her. It started as a tingling at the base of her skull, a prickle of awareness that something was wrong, something she couldn't quite put her finger on. The room around her seemed to shift, the edges of her vision blurring, as if reality itself were beginning to unravel.

Sarah blinked, her heart rate quickening as she tried to focus on her surroundings. But the more she tried to ground herself, the more distorted everything became. The walls seemed to pulse with a life of their own, the shadows growing darker, more oppressive, until they threatened to swallow her whole.

Her breath hitched, and she set the cup of tea down on the table, her hands trembling. "This isn't real," she whispered to herself, her voice shaky. "It's just... stress. It's all in my head."

But even as she said the words, she knew they weren't true. Something was happening, something beyond her control, and it was terrifying in its intensity.

And then, she heard it—a voice, soft and mournful, echoing through the room.

"Why didn't you save me, Sarah?"

The words were a dagger to her heart, slicing through her composure and leaving her reeling. She knew that voice, recognized it instantly, though she hadn't heard it in years.

"Why didn't you do more?"

Sarah gasped, her hand flying to her mouth as she realized what was happening. It was the patient—the one she had lost, the one who had taken their own life after Sarah had failed to recognize the signs of their deepening depression.

"No... no, this isn't real," Sarah whispered, her voice trembling with fear. "You're not here... you're gone."

But the voice persisted, growing louder, more insistent, as if it were coming from within her own mind.

"You could have saved me. You should have saved me."

Sarah's vision blurred, her heart pounding in her chest as she tried to block out the voice, to push it away. But it was relentless, the echo of her guilt manifesting in a way that she had never experienced before.

She stumbled to her feet, her legs unsteady as she tried to escape the sound, but it followed her, growing louder with each step she took. The walls of her home seemed to close in around her, the shadows stretching out like fingers, reaching for her, pulling her deeper into the nightmare.

"No!" Sarah cried, her voice breaking as she clutched her head, trying to block out the sound. "I'm sorry... I'm so sorry..."

The air in the room grew thick, suffocating, as if the very atmosphere had turned against her. The voice was all around her now, echoing off the walls, filling her mind with images of the patient she had lost—their face twisted in despair, their eyes filled with pain that she hadn't been able to see until it was too late.

"You didn't listen. You didn't care."

Sarah fell to her knees, her body trembling as the echo of her guilt consumed her. The memories of that time, memories she had buried deep within herself, came flooding back, overwhelming her with their intensity. The long nights spent worrying about the patient, the growing sense of dread as she realized she was losing them, the crushing weight of failure when she found out they had taken their own life—it all came rushing back, dragging her down into the darkness.

Tears streamed down her face as she clutched her head, the sound of the voice reverberating through her skull. She couldn't escape it, couldn't outrun it. It was a part of her, a manifestation of the guilt and shame that had been festering inside her for years.

And then, just as suddenly as it had begun, the echo stopped. The voice faded away, leaving Sarah gasping for breath in the silence that followed.

She knelt on the floor, her body shaking, her mind reeling from the experience. The room around her was calm once more, the shadows retreating, the walls solid and unmoving. But the peace that had once filled her home was gone, replaced by a deep, gnawing sense of dread.

Sarah took a shaky breath, her hand trembling as she wiped the tears from her face. She had always prided herself on her rationality, on her ability to keep a clear head even in the most difficult of circumstances. But now, in the aftermath of the echo, she felt as though she had been stripped bare, her deepest fears and regrets laid out for the world to see.

She stood up slowly, her legs unsteady as she made her way back to the armchair. The cup of tea sat on the table, cold and untouched, a stark reminder of the calm she had so desperately sought.

But there would be no more calm, no more peace—not now, not after what she had experienced.

Sarah sank into the chair, her mind racing as she tried to make sense of what had just happened. The echo had been so real, so vivid, that it had shattered her perception of reality, leaving her questioning everything she had ever known.

And in that moment, Sarah realized that she could no longer dismiss what Aaron had told her. The echoes, the force that was growing stronger in Whistler's Grove—it was real, and it was far more powerful than she had ever imagined.

She had been a skeptic, someone who believed only in what she could see and touch. But now, after experiencing the echo for herself, she knew that there were forces at work that defied explanation, forces that were rooted in the darkest corners of the human mind.

And those forces were coming for them all.

Sarah's thoughts turned to Aaron, to the darkness he had been battling, and she felt a deep sense of dread settle over her. If the echoes could do this to her, someone who had always prided herself on her rationality, what were they doing to him? How much more could

he take before the darkness consumed him completely?

She couldn't let that happen. She couldn't stand by and watch as the people she cared about were destroyed by forces they didn't understand.

Sarah took a deep breath, her resolve hardening. She had always been a protector, someone who cared deeply for her patients, for her friends. And now, as she faced the darkness that had taken hold of her mind, she knew that she couldn't turn away from it.

She had to confront it, had to find a way to fight back against the forces that were threatening to tear them all apart.

But first, she had to accept the truth—that the world was not as orderly and controlled as she had always believed. There were things in this world, things beyond her understanding, that could reach into the very depths of a person's soul and twist it into something dark and unrecognizable.

And those things were real. They were here, in Whistler's Grove, and they were growing stronger with each passing day.

Sarah stood up, her mind clear for the first time since the echo had taken hold. She wasn't the same person she had been before—she couldn't be. The echo had changed her, had forced her to confront the darkest parts of herself, and in doing so, it had opened her eyes to the reality of the world around her.

She was no longer a skeptic. She was a believer, and that belief filled her with a sense of purpose, a determination to uncover the truth and to protect the people she cared about from the darkness that was closing in on them.

Sarah looked around her home, at the calm and order that she had once taken comfort in, and realized that it was nothing more than an illusion. The real world was chaotic, unpredictable, filled with forces that she could barely comprehend.

And it was up to her to face those forces, to confront the darkness, and to find a way to bring light back into their lives.

She grabbed her coat, the determination in her eyes burning bright as she headed for the door. She had work to do, and there was no time to waste.

The darkness was growing, the echoes were getting louder, and if they didn't act soon, it would consume them all.

But Sarah was ready. She was no longer afraid of the shadows, no longer running from the guilt and shame that had haunted her for so long.

She was ready to fight back, to face the darkness head-on, and to find a way to banish it once and for all.

And she knew that she wouldn't be alone. Aaron, Elena, Mark—they were all in this together, all fighting the same battle, and together, they would find a way to defeat the force that was threatening to destroy them.

Because they had to. There was no other choice.

Chapter 12: The Legacy of Shadows

Aaron Blake's hands trembled as he pushed open the door to his father's hidden study. The old, weathered wood creaked under the pressure, revealing a room that had been sealed away from the world for decades. The air inside was thick, stale, with a faint scent of decay that hinted at the secrets buried within. The room itself was dark, the only light coming from the flickering flames of the candles that lined the walls, casting long, wavering shadows that danced across the floor.

The study was exactly as Aaron remembered it from his childhood, yet it felt entirely different now, as if the years of neglect had transformed it into something darker, something more sinister. The room was filled with relics of a past that Aaron had tried desperately to forget—shelves lined with dusty books, old medical instruments arranged with precision, and strange, arcane symbols etched into the walls and floor.

He took a step inside, his breath catching in his throat as the memories came flooding back. He had been just a boy the last time he was in this room, a boy who had idolized his father, who had believed that everything Richard Blake did was for the greater good. But now, standing here as a man, Aaron knew better. The things his father had done in this room, the experiments he had conducted—they were the source of the darkness that had been unleashed on Whistler's Grove, the darkness that now threatened to consume them all.

Aaron's gaze drifted to the far side of the room, where a large, intricately carved desk sat, covered in papers and medical charts. The desk had always been his father's sanctuary, the place where he had spent hours poring over his research, scribbling notes in his indecipherable handwriting. But now, as Aaron approached it, he could feel the weight of the secrets it held pressing down on him, threatening to crush him under their burden.

He reached out, his fingers brushing against the worn leather of the chair that stood behind the desk, and a chill ran down his spine. His father's presence lingered in this room, as if the man himself were standing just behind him, watching, waiting for the moment when his son would finally uncover the truth.

Aaron hesitated, his heart pounding in his chest. He didn't want to do this. He didn't want to know what his father had done, didn't want to face the reality of the man he had once revered. But he knew he had no choice. The answers he needed were here, in this room, hidden among the relics of a past that had been carefully concealed from him.

With a deep breath, Aaron reached for the first of the many journals that littered the desk. The leather-bound book was old, the pages yellowed with age, and as he opened it, a cloud of dust rose into the air, making him cough. The writing inside was meticulous, the lines of text cramped and precise, written in a hand that Aaron knew all too well—his father's.

The first entries were clinical, detailing the day-to-day operations of the asylum, the treatments administered, the progress of various patients. But as Aaron flipped through the pages, the tone began to shift, the entries growing darker, more erratic, as his father delved deeper into his research.

Aaron's eyes scanned the pages, his heart sinking as he read the words that had been hidden from him for so long. His father's research had started out with noble intentions—a desire to understand the human mind, to find a cure for the mental illnesses that plagued so many. But somewhere along the way, that desire had twisted into something far more dangerous.

The entries detailed experiments that went far beyond the bounds of ethical science—experiments that involved rituals, occult symbols, and the manipulation of forces that Aaron could barely comprehend. His father had become obsessed with the idea of opening a doorway, a gateway to another realm, one that he believed held the key to unlocking the true potential of the human mind.

But the gateway his father had opened hadn't led to enlightenment. It had led to darkness.

Aaron's hands shook as he turned the pages, the full extent of his father's actions becoming horrifyingly clear. The experiments had been conducted on patients who had been deemed too far gone to save—people who had been locked away in the asylum, forgotten by the world. His father had used them as test subjects, pushing them to the brink of madness in his quest to tap into the echoes, the memories of past lives, the voices of the dead.

And then there was the final entry, the one that made Aaron's blood run cold.

"Experiment No. 47—Subject: Margaret Carter. Heightened sensitivity to echoes detected. Further exploration of family lineage required. Possible connection to ancestral trauma linked to malevolent force. Proceed with caution."

Margaret Carter. The name leaped off the page, sending a jolt of recognition through Aaron. He knew that name. Elena's family name was Carter, and the connection between them could no longer be ignored.

His father had been aware of Elena's family history, of the curse that had followed them for generations. He had used Margaret as a key in his experiments, probing her mind, trying to unlock the secrets of her past, of the echoes that had haunted her. And in doing so, he had unleashed something far darker than he had ever anticipated.

Aaron's hands tightened around the edges of the journal, his breath coming in ragged gasps. The truth was unbearable. His father hadn't just been a man of science—he had been a man consumed by his own hubris, willing to sacrifice innocent lives in his quest for power and knowledge. And now, the sins of the father were being visited upon the son.

He slammed the journal shut, his chest heaving as he struggled to control the rage and despair that threatened to overwhelm him. How could he have been so blind? How could he have ever believed that his father was a good man, that the work he had done was anything other than monstrous?

Aaron's gaze drifted around the room, taking in the symbols etched into the walls, the medical instruments stained with the blood of his father's victims. This was his legacy—the legacy of a man who had delved too deeply into the darkness, who had brought a curse down upon his own bloodline.

The sound of footsteps behind him made Aaron turn, and he saw Elena standing in the doorway, her face pale, her eyes wide with shock.

"Aaron," she whispered, her voice trembling. "What is this place?"

Aaron looked at her, his heart breaking at the fear and confusion in her eyes. He had dragged her into this, had brought her to this place of nightmares, and now she was caught up in the web of darkness that his father had woven.

"This was my father's study," Aaron said, his voice hollow. "This is where he conducted his experiments... where he unleashed the force that's been haunting us."

Elena took a step closer, her gaze drifting to the symbols on the walls, the strange instruments that lined the shelves. "He was... involved in the occult?"

Aaron nodded, the weight of the truth pressing down on him like a physical force. "He believed that by tapping into the echoes—the memories of the dead—he could open a doorway to another realm. He thought it would lead to enlightenment, but instead... he unleashed something far worse."

Elena's eyes filled with tears, her voice choked with emotion. "And my family... Margaret Carter... she was one of his test subjects?"

Aaron looked away, unable to meet her gaze. "Yes. He believed that your family's history, the trauma that had been passed down through the generations, was the key to unlocking the full potential of his experiments. But he was wrong, Elena. He was so wrong."

Elena's hands shook as she reached out to touch one of the symbols on the wall, her fingers tracing the intricate lines. "So this... all of this... it's because of what your father did?"

Aaron felt a deep sense of guilt and shame wash over him, a burden that he knew he would carry for the rest of his life. "Yes. My father's actions led to the horrors we're facing now. And I'm so sorry, Elena. I'm sorry that you're caught up in this, that my father's sins have become your burden."

Elena turned to him, her eyes filled with a mix of fear and determination. "It's not your fault, Aaron. You're not responsible for what your father did. But we have to find a way to stop this... before it consumes us all."

Aaron nodded, but the weight of his father's legacy pressed down on him like a heavy shroud. How could he ever escape it? How could he ever make amends for the darkness that his father had unleashed?

He turned back to the desk, his eyes drawn to a small, locked box that sat in the corner. It was old, made of dark wood, and intricately carved with symbols that matched the ones on the walls. Aaron had seen this box before, had watched his father lock it away, hiding it from prying eyes. Whatever was inside, Aaron knew it held the key to understanding the full extent of his father's involvement in the occult.

With shaking hands, Aaron reached for the box, his fingers brushing against the cold metal of the lock. It was rusted with age, but it gave way easily under his touch, the lid creaking open to reveal its contents.

Inside the box was a single, yellowed piece of paper, covered in his father's neat, precise handwriting. Aaron's breath caught in his throat as he unfolded it, his eyes scanning the words that would forever change his understanding of his father's legacy.

"Final Experiment—The Binding Ritual. Success depends on the subject's ability to harness the echoes and control the malevolent force. Failure

will result in the complete destruction of the subject's mind and soul. Risk must be weighed against potential rewards. The Carter lineage shows promise, but caution is advised."

Aaron's hands shook as he read the words, the full horror of his father's final experiment dawning on him. His father had planned to bind the malevolent force to a living host, to control it, to use it as a tool for his own gain. And he had chosen Margaret Carter as his test subject.

But something had gone wrong—terribly wrong. The ritual had failed, and instead of controlling the force, his father had unleashed it, setting it free to wreak havoc on the world.

Aaron's knees gave out, and he sank to the floor, the weight of the revelation too much to bear. This was his father's legacy—a legacy of madness, of hubris, of destruction. And now, that legacy had fallen to him.

Elena knelt beside him, her hand resting on his shoulder. "Aaron, we can't change the past. But we can fight for the future. We can find a way to stop this, to end the cycle of darkness."

Aaron looked up at her, his heart heavy with guilt and despair. "How, Elena? How can we fight something that's been growing in power for decades? Something that's already taken so much from us?"

Elena's eyes were fierce, determined. "We fight it with everything we have. We fight it together. Your father's actions may have started this, but we can end it. We have to believe that."

Aaron wanted to believe her, wanted to cling to the hope that they could find a way to stop the darkness that had taken root in Whistler's Grove. But the weight of his father's sins was a heavy burden to bear, one that threatened to crush him under its weight.

He looked around the study, at the symbols etched into the walls, the medical instruments that had been used in the experiments, the journals that detailed the descent into madness. This was his inheritance, the legacy of a man who had been consumed by his own ambition, who had sacrificed everything in his quest for power.

But it didn't have to be his future. He didn't have to follow in his father's footsteps. He could make a different choice, could fight against the darkness, could find a way to bring light back into the world.

Aaron took a deep breath, his resolve hardening. He wouldn't let his father's sins define him. He would fight, alongside Elena, alongside Mark and Sarah, to end the darkness that had been unleashed.

He stood up, his eyes meeting Elena's. "You're right. We can't let this force win. We have to find a way to stop it, to break the cycle."

Elena nodded, her expression filled with determination. "We will, Aaron. We'll do whatever it takes."

As they left the study, Aaron couldn't shake the feeling that his father's presence was still there, watching, waiting. The legacy of Richard Blake was a dark one, but it was a legacy that Aaron was determined to overcome.

They stepped out into the night, the cool air a stark contrast to the oppressive atmosphere of the study. The stars above twinkled in the sky, distant and untouchable, a reminder that there was still light in the world, still hope.

Aaron looked back at the house, at the dark windows that stared back at him like empty eyes. The shadows of the past were deep, but they were not insurmountable.

And with that thought, Aaron turned away from the house, his steps firm as he and Elena walked into the night, ready to face whatever darkness lay ahead.

Chapter 13: Bloodlines of Shadows

The library was quiet, its silence broken only by the soft rustle of paper as Aaron and Elena flipped through the dusty volumes and old records that lined the shelves. The room was dimly lit, the only source of light coming from a single, flickering lamp on the large wooden table where they sat. Shadows danced on the walls, and the air was thick with the scent of old books and aging paper—a smell that spoke of secrets long buried, of history forgotten.

Elena sat across from Aaron, her brow furrowed in concentration as she pored over the ancient documents spread out before her. Her fingers trembled slightly as she turned the pages, each one revealing more about her family's dark past, about the secrets that had been hidden from her for so long.

The library itself was an old building, tucked away in a forgotten corner of Whistler's Grove, its walls lined with shelves that held the town's history—the history that no one wanted to remember. The librarian had given them a wary look when they had arrived, but she hadn't asked any questions, simply guiding them to the back of the library where the oldest records were kept, and then leaving them alone with their search.

Elena's heart pounded in her chest as she uncovered more and more about her great-grandfather, Johnathan Carter. The records were fragmented, incomplete, but they painted a chilling picture of a man who had been deeply involved in the same experiments that Aaron's father had conducted. The experiments that had unleashed the malevolent force that now threatened to consume them all.

She looked up at Aaron, who was engrossed in his own research, his face set in a grim expression as he read through the notes left behind by the men who had once worked alongside his father. The silence between them was heavy, filled with the weight of the knowledge they were uncovering—the knowledge that would forever change their understanding of themselves, of the town, of the darkness that had taken root in their lives.

Elena's gaze drifted back to the document in front of her, her eyes scanning the faded ink as she tried to make sense of what she was reading. It was a journal entry, dated nearly a century ago, written by Johnathan Carter himself. The words were cryptic, but they spoke of something that chilled her to the bone—an experiment that had gone terribly wrong, an experiment that had bound the echoes to the Carter bloodline.

She shivered as she read the entry, her mind racing. Her great-grandfather had been involved in the same experiments as Aaron's father, and the results had been catastrophic. The echoes, the malevolent force—they weren't just random occurrences. They were tied to her family, to her bloodline, passed down from generation to generation like a curse.

"Elena," Aaron's voice broke through her thoughts, drawing her attention back to him. He looked up from the document he was reading, his eyes meeting hers with a mixture of concern and understanding. "I think I've found something."

She leaned closer, her heart pounding with a mix of fear and anticipation. "What is it?"

Aaron held up the document, a yellowed piece of paper covered in his father's familiar handwriting. "It's a letter—written by my father to Johnathan Carter. He talks about the experiments they were conducting together, about how they believed they could harness the power of the echoes, use them to access some kind of... otherworldly knowledge."

Elena's breath caught in her throat. "Otherworldly knowledge?"

Aaron nodded, his expression grim. "They thought the echoes were more than just memories, that they were a connection to something beyond our world—a realm where the dead and the living could intersect, where time itself had no meaning. They believed that by tapping into this realm, they could gain insight into the deepest mysteries of the universe."

Elena felt a chill run down her spine. The echoes had always been a part of her life, a strange and unsettling presence that she could never fully understand. But now, as she listened to Aaron's words, she realized that the echoes were more than just random occurrences—they were a manifestation of something far darker, something that had been passed down through her family, twisted and corrupted by the experiments her great-grandfather and Aaron's father had conducted.

"They thought they could control it," Aaron continued, his voice heavy with the weight of his own guilt. "But they were wrong. The echoes weren't something that could be harnessed or controlled. They were a force, a living entity, tied to the souls of the dead, and by trying to manipulate them, they unleashed something far more dangerous than they ever anticipated."

Elena stared at the document in Aaron's hand, her mind reeling. "And my great-grandfather... he was a part of this?"

Aaron nodded, his gaze somber. "He was one of the key figures in the experiments. From what I've read, he was the one who first discovered the connection between the echoes and the Carter bloodline. He believed that your family had a unique sensitivity to the echoes, that the trauma passed down through your ancestors had somehow amplified their power."

Elena felt a deep sense of dread settle over her. The echoes, the nightmares that had haunted her for so long—they weren't just a random occurrence. They were a part of her, a part of her family's legacy, passed down from generation to generation like a curse.

She took a deep breath, trying to steady herself. "But why? Why did they think they could control it?"

Aaron hesitated, his eyes dark with something she couldn't quite decipher. "I think they believed they could use the echoes to access some kind of higher power, something that would give them the ability to reshape reality itself. They thought they could use it for good, to heal the mind, to cure mental illness. But in their hubris, they didn't realize the danger they were playing with."

Elena's mind raced as she tried to process what Aaron was saying. The echoes, the force that had been unleashed—they were all connected to her family, to the experiments that her great-grandfather had been a part of. The weight of that knowledge pressed down on her, suffocating her, but at the same time, it brought a strange sense of clarity.

"I'm connected to this, aren't I?" she whispered, her voice trembling with a mixture of fear and determination. "I'm connected to the echoes... to the force."

Aaron reached out, his hand covering hers, his touch grounding her in the midst of the storm raging in her mind. "Yes, you are. But that doesn't mean you're powerless. If anything, it means you might be the only one who can stop it."

Elena's eyes widened, her breath catching in her throat. "Stop it? How? How can I stop something that's been growing in power for generations?"

Aaron squeezed her hand, his voice firm. "Because you're the key, Elena. The connection between your family and the echoes—it's stronger than anything my father or your great-grandfather ever anticipated. But that also means you have the potential to control it, to harness that power and use it to destroy the force before it destroys us."

Elena stared at him, her mind racing. Control the echoes? Harness their power? The very idea seemed impossible, but as she looked into

Aaron's eyes, she saw the conviction there, the belief that she was capable of something far greater than she had ever imagined.

"But what if I fail?" she whispered, her voice filled with doubt. "What if I make things worse?"

Aaron's expression softened, his voice gentle as he spoke. "You won't fail, Elena. You're stronger than you realize. And you're not alone in this. We're in this together, and we'll find a way to stop this, to end the cycle of darkness."

Elena wanted to believe him, wanted to cling to the hope that she could be the one to break the curse that had plagued her family for so long. But the weight of her newfound knowledge was heavy, and the responsibility that came with it was almost too much to bear.

She pulled her hand away from Aaron's, her gaze drifting back to the document in front of her. The words blurred as tears filled her eyes, the enormity of her situation crashing down on her like a wave. Her great-grandfather's actions had set this all in motion, and now it was up to her to stop it.

But how could she, a mere mortal, stand against a force that had been growing in power for decades? A force that was rooted in the very fabric of her being, a part of her bloodline?

Elena's thoughts turned to the stories she had heard as a child, stories passed down through her family about the old country, about the curses that had followed them across the ocean, curses that were born of ancient grudges and unholy pacts. She had always dismissed them as just that—stories, tales meant to frighten children and keep them in line. But now, she realized that those stories held a grain of truth, a truth that had been twisted and distorted over the generations, but a truth nonetheless.

Her family had been cursed, not by some vengeful spirit or angry god, but by the actions of their ancestors, by the choices they had made in the pursuit of power. And that curse had been passed down, from parent to child, each generation inheriting the sins of the ones that came before.

But just as the curse had been passed down, so too had the potential to break it. Elena could feel it now, deep within her—an energy, a power that she had never fully understood but that had always been a part of her. It was the same power that had allowed her to hear the echoes, to feel the presence of the dead, to connect with the spirits that lingered in the world

of the living.

It was a power that had been twisted and corrupted by her great-grandfather's experiments, but it was still there, still hers, and it was growing stronger.

Elena took a deep breath, her resolve hardening as she realized what she had to do. She couldn't run from this, couldn't hide from the responsibility that had been placed on her shoulders. She had to face it, to embrace the power within her and use it to fight back against the darkness that had been unleashed.

She looked up at Aaron, her eyes filled with a newfound determination. "We need to find out more," she said, her voice steady. "If I'm the key to stopping this, then we need to understand exactly what my great-grandfather did, how he bound the echoes to our family. There has to be something here, in these records, that can help us."

Aaron nodded, his own determination matching hers. "You're right. We need to keep digging, to find any information we can that might help us figure out how to stop this. My father's notes, your great-grandfather's journal—there has to be something that can give us a clue."

They spent the next several hours combing through the old records, searching for any scrap of information that might give them the answers they needed. The flickering light of the lamp cast long shadows across the room, but neither of them noticed the passage of time, so focused were they on their task.

Finally, after what felt like an eternity, Elena found something—a document, hidden away in the back of a dusty old book, written in her great-grandfather's hand. It was a ritual, detailed and precise, describing the steps he had taken to bind the echoes to his bloodline, to harness their power for his own purposes.

Elena's hands shook as she read the words, her heart pounding in her chest. This was it—this was the key to everything. Her great-grandfather had believed that by binding the echoes to his bloodline, he could control them, use them to gain the knowledge and power he so desperately sought. But in doing so, he had also bound his descendants to the echoes, to the malevolent force that had been growing stronger with each generation.

Aaron leaned over her shoulder, his eyes scanning the document. "This is it," he said, his voice filled with a mixture of awe and fear. "This is how it all started."

Elena nodded, her mind racing. "And this... this is how we end it. If my great-grandfather was able to bind the echoes, then maybe I can find a way to unbind them, to break the connection and destroy the force once and for all."

Aaron looked at her, his eyes filled with hope. "You can do this, Elena. I know you can. We'll figure this out together."

Elena's heart swelled with a mixture of fear and determination. The task ahead of her was daunting, terrifying even, but she knew that she had to try. She had to find a way to break the curse that had plagued her family for so long, to destroy the force that had taken so much from them.

She looked back at the ritual, her mind already working through the details, trying to understand what her great-grandfather had done and how she could reverse it. The power within her, the connection to the echoes, was both a blessing and a curse, but it was also the key to their salvation.

Elena took a deep breath, her resolve hardening. She was ready. Ready to face the darkness, ready to embrace the power within her, ready to break the cycle of destruction that had been set in motion so many years ago.

She looked up at Aaron, her eyes filled with a steely determination. "Let's do this," she said, her voice strong and unwavering. "Let's end this once and for all."

Aaron nodded, his expression matching hers. "Together."

As they left the library, the old records and dusty books behind them, Elena felt a sense of purpose that she had never felt before. The road ahead would be difficult, fraught with danger and uncertainty, but she knew that she wasn't alone. She had Aaron by her side, and together, they would find a way to end the darkness that had plagued their lives for so long.

Because they had to. There was no other choice.

Chapter 14: Echoes of the Past

The town's archive was a forgotten corner of Whistler's Grove, tucked away in the basement of the old courthouse, where dust-covered shelves groaned under the weight of centuries of history. The air was musty and thick, the scent of decaying paper mingling with the faint odor of mildew. It was a place that few people visited, a relic of the past that had been left to rot along with the memories it held.

Mark Harris stood in the doorway, his eyes scanning the dimly lit room. The shelves were crammed with boxes of documents, old maps, and yellowed newspapers, all jumbled together in a chaotic mess. It was the kind of place where secrets could be easily lost, buried under the weight of time, hidden from the eyes of those who didn't know where to look.

But Mark knew what he was looking for. He had spent the past few days piecing together the fragments of information he had gathered from the crime scenes, from Aaron's revelations, and from his own investigation. All the clues pointed to the same place: Shadowbrook Asylum, the dark heart of Whistler's Grove.

The asylum had been shut down decades ago, its history buried along with the bodies of the patients who had suffered and died within its walls. But Mark knew that the past had a way of resurfacing, that the echoes of old sins could never truly be silenced. And now, those echoes were back, bringing with them a darkness that threatened to consume everything in its path.

Mark walked deeper into the archive, his footsteps echoing off the concrete floor. The fluorescent lights flickered overhead, casting eerie shadows that seemed to dance on the walls, following him as he made his way through the narrow aisles. He could feel the weight of the past pressing down on him, the oppressive silence broken only by the occasional creak of the building settling around him.

He reached the back of the room, where the oldest records were kept, and began his search. The files were dusty, their labels faded and illegible, but Mark didn't let that deter him. He was a detective, and he knew how to find the truth, even when it was buried under layers of neglect.

He pulled out a box labeled "Shadowbrook Asylum" and placed it on the nearby table, the wood creaking under the weight. The box was old, the cardboard brittle, and as Mark lifted the lid, a cloud of dust rose into the air, making him cough.

Inside, he found a collection of documents—patient records, incident reports, and correspondences, all haphazardly thrown together. But it wasn't the official records that caught Mark's attention. It was a stack of yellowed papers, tied together with a frayed piece of twine, that looked as if they had been hidden away deliberately, their edges browned with age, the ink faded.

Mark untied the twine and began to read, his brow furrowing as the words on the page slowly revealed the dark history of the asylum, and the land it had been built on.

The asylum had been constructed in the late 1800s, during a time when Whistler's Grove was little more than a small farming community. The land had been purchased by a group of wealthy investors who had been drawn to the area by its isolation, its remoteness from the rest of the world. They had seen it as the perfect place to build a facility where they could conduct their experiments, free from the prying eyes of the public.

But the land they had chosen was not an ordinary piece of property. It had a history, one that was steeped in blood and tragedy. According to the documents Mark was reading, the land had once been the site of a mass tragedy, a massacre that had taken place long before the town of Whistler's Grove had been founded.

The papers told the story of a small Native American village that had once stood on the land, a peaceful community that had lived there for generations. But in the early 1700s, during a particularly harsh winter, a group of settlers had come to the village, desperate for food and shelter. The villagers had taken them in, sharing what little they had, but the settlers had turned on them, slaughtering the entire village in a single night.

The massacre had been brutal, the ground soaked with the blood of men, women, and children. The settlers had taken the land for themselves, but they had never prospered. Crops had withered, livestock had died, and one by one, the settlers had succumbed to madness, taking their own lives or turning on each other in fits of violence.

The land had been abandoned, left to the elements, until the investors had purchased it over a century later, unaware of its dark history. But the curse had never lifted, the blood that had been spilled seeping into the soil, tainting it, corrupting it.

And then the asylum had been built, and the curse had taken on a new form.

The documents revealed that the founders of the asylum had been aware of the land's history, but they had dismissed it as mere superstition. They had been men of science, men who believed in progress and rationality, and they had seen the stories as nothing more than the remnants of a primitive belief system. But they had been wrong.

As the asylum grew, as more patients were admitted, the darkness that had lain dormant in the land began to awaken. The echoes of the past, the memories of the massacre, had become intertwined with the suffering of the patients, feeding off their pain, their fear, growing stronger with each passing year.

Mark's hands trembled as he read the words, the full horror of what had been unleashed on the town of Whistler's Grove becoming clear. The malevolent force that Aaron and Elena had been battling—it wasn't just a product of the experiments conducted at the asylum. It was something far older, something that had been born out of the bloodshed that had taken place on the land centuries ago.

The force had been growing in power ever since, feeding off the echoes of the past, using the asylum as a conduit to spread its influence. And now, it had set its sights on Aaron and Elena, the two people who were most closely connected to the asylum's dark history.

Mark felt a cold knot of fear settle in his stomach. Aaron and Elena weren't just fighting against the echoes—they were fighting against a force that had been born out of unimaginable tragedy, a force that had been growing in power for centuries, feeding off the pain and suffering of the people who had lived and died on the cursed land.

He had to warn them. He had to make them understand the true depth of the threat they were facing. The force wasn't just a product of the asylum's experiments—it was something far older, far more powerful, and it wasn't going to stop until it had claimed them as its next victims.

Mark quickly gathered up the documents, shoving them into his bag. He couldn't waste any more time. He had to get to Aaron and Elena, had to tell them what he had discovered. Their lives depended on it.

As he made his way out of the archive, his mind raced. The pieces were finally starting to come together, the full scope of the darkness that had been unleashed on Whistler's Grove becoming clear. The asylum, the land, the echoes—it was all connected, all part of the same twisted web of tragedy and pain.

But there was still one question that remained unanswered: how could they stop it?

The force had been growing in power for centuries, feeding off the pain and suffering of generations. It was rooted in the very land itself, a product of the blood that had been spilled so many years ago. How could they hope to fight something that was so deeply entrenched in the fabric of the town, something that had been growing stronger with each passing year?

Mark didn't have the answers, but he knew one thing for certain: they couldn't fight this battle alone. They needed to find a way to break the cycle, to sever the connection between the force and the land, to destroy the echoes before they consumed everything.

As he stepped out into the cool night air, Mark felt a sense of urgency gnawing at him. Time was running out, and the force was closing in on them. They had to act quickly, had to find a way to stop the darkness before it was too late.

Mark climbed into his car, his mind racing as he drove through the quiet streets of Whistler's Grove. The town seemed peaceful, the houses dark, the streets empty, but Mark knew better. The darkness was there, lurking just beneath the surface, waiting for the right moment to strike.

He pulled up to Aaron's house, his heart pounding in his chest. The lights were on inside, a warm glow spilling out onto the porch, but Mark felt no comfort in the sight. He knew that the battle they were about to face would be unlike anything they had ever encountered before.

Mark hurried up the steps, his breath misting in the cool night air as he knocked on the door. A moment later, Aaron opened it, his expression tense, his eyes filled with worry.

"Mark," Aaron said, his voice tight. "What's going on?"

Mark stepped inside, his gaze flicking to Elena, who was sitting on the couch, her face pale, her eyes wide with fear. She looked up at him, her expression pleading, as if she already knew that the news he was bringing wasn't good.

"I found something," Mark said, his voice urgent. "In the town archive. The asylum—it's not just about the experiments. It's the land itself. It's cursed, Aaron. There was a massacre, long before the asylum was built. The blood that was spilled—it tainted the land, created a darkness that's been growing ever since."

Aaron's eyes widened, his

expression darkening as the weight of Mark's words sank in. "The land… it's been feeding the force?"

Mark nodded, his heart heavy with the knowledge he had uncovered. "Yes. And the echoes—they're not just memories. They're the remnants of that darkness, the pain and suffering of the people who died there. The asylum, the experiments—they only made it stronger, gave it a way to spread, to infect the town."

Elena's hands trembled as she listened, her voice barely above a whisper. "And now it's coming for us."

Mark's gaze flicked between Aaron and Elena, his heart pounding in his chest. "Yes. You're both connected to the asylum, to the force. You're the last pieces of the puzzle, the last echoes that it needs to complete its cycle. And it's not going to stop until it has you."

The room fell silent, the weight of Mark's revelation pressing down on them like a physical force. They were facing something far more powerful, far more ancient, than they had ever imagined. A darkness that had been growing for centuries, feeding off the pain and suffering of the people of Whistler's Grove.

But despite the fear that gnawed at the edges of his mind, Mark felt a flicker of determination ignite within him. They had come too far, uncovered too much, to give up now. They had to find a way to stop the force, to break the cycle of darkness that had been plaguing the town for so long.

"We're not going to let it win," Mark said, his voice filled with conviction. "We're going to fight it, together. We'll find a way to stop the echoes, to sever the connection between the force and the land. We have to."

Aaron nodded, his jaw clenched with determination. "We will. We've come too far to back down now."

Elena looked between the two of them, her fear giving way to a steely resolve. "We'll do whatever it takes. We'll end this."

As they stood together in the small living room, the darkness of the past pressing in on them from all sides, they knew that the battle ahead would be their greatest challenge yet. But they also knew that they had no other choice.

The force was coming for them, and they had to be ready.

Chapter 15: The Final Confrontation

The night was thick with fog, the kind that seemed to cling to the skin and swallow the light whole. The road leading to Shadowbrook Asylum was a winding, narrow path, barely visible through the mist that curled around the trees like ghostly tendrils. The headlights of Aaron's car cut through the darkness, illuminating the twisted branches that arched over the road like skeletal fingers reaching out of the abyss.

Inside the car, the tension was palpable. Aaron gripped the steering wheel, his knuckles white, his breath shallow and controlled. Beside him, Elena sat silently, her gaze fixed on the road ahead, her mind racing with the knowledge of what awaited them. In the back seat, Mark and Sarah exchanged glances, both of them acutely aware of the danger they were heading into but determined to see it through.

As they approached the asylum, the building loomed out of the fog, a hulking shadow against the night sky. It stood like a monument to madness, its stone walls covered in creeping vines, its windows dark and lifeless. The structure seemed to pulse with a malevolent energy, as if the very ground it stood on was poisoned by the horrors that had taken place within its walls.

Aaron slowed the car as they reached the gate, the iron bars rusted and bent, the chains that once held it shut long broken. The gate creaked open with a groan, as if protesting their intrusion, but Aaron pressed on, guiding the car up the long, winding drive toward the entrance.

They stepped out of the car into the cold, damp night, the fog swirling around their feet as they approached the massive oak doors of the asylum. The air was thick with the scent of damp earth and decay, and the silence was oppressive, broken only by the distant rustle of leaves and the faint whisper of the wind.

Aaron looked back at the others, his expression grim. "This is it," he said, his voice low and steady. "Whatever happens in there... we face it together."

Elena nodded, her resolve hardening as she looked up at the asylum, the place where her family's curse had been born, where the echoes had been twisted into something dark and malevolent. "We end this tonight," she said, her voice filled with a quiet determination.

Mark and Sarah exchanged a glance, both of them feeling the weight of the moment. They had come too far, uncovered too much, to turn back now. Whatever awaited them inside, they would face it head-on.

Aaron pushed open the doors, the wood groaning under the pressure, and they stepped inside, the darkness swallowing them whole.

The interior of the asylum was a labyrinth of crumbling hallways and decaying rooms, the walls covered in peeling paint and mold, the floors littered with debris. The air was heavy, thick with the scent of rot and something else—something darker, more sinister. The building seemed to hum with a low, almost imperceptible vibration, as if it were alive, as if it were aware of their presence.

They moved cautiously through the halls, the beam of their flashlights cutting through the darkness, revealing glimpses of the asylum's twisted past. Old medical instruments lay scattered across the floors, rusted and broken. Patient records, their pages yellowed with age, were strewn about, their contents long forgotten. And everywhere, there were the echoes—faint, distant whispers that seemed to come from the walls themselves, growing louder the deeper they ventured into the heart of the asylum.

As they reached the central atrium, the echoes became a cacophony of voices, each one filled with pain, fear, and anger. The air seemed to pulse with the weight of their collective suffering, the shadows stretching and twisting in unnatural ways.

Aaron stopped in the center of the room, his heart pounding in his chest. He could feel it—the force, the malevolent entity that had been growing stronger with each passing day. It was here, waiting for them, feeding off the darkness that had taken root in this place, feeding off their fear and guilt.

"It's close," Aaron said, his voice barely above a whisper.

Elena nodded, her hand tightening around the small, leather-bound journal she had brought with her—the journal that had once belonged to her great-grandfather, the man who had set all of this in motion. The journal contained the ritual he had used to bind the echoes to their bloodline, the ritual that had unleashed the malevolent force. And now, it was the key to their salvation.

They moved deeper into the asylum, the air growing colder with each step, the shadows closing in around them. The echoes grew louder, more insistent, the voices merging into a single, overwhelming roar that threatened to drown out all reason.

And then, they reached it—the heart of the asylum, the place where the final experiment had been conducted. The room was large, the walls lined with arcane symbols, the floor covered in a circle of blood that had long since dried to a dark, rust-colored stain. The center of the circle was marked by an altar, a crude stone slab that seemed to pulse with a faint, unnatural light.

Aaron's breath caught in his throat as he looked around the room, the weight of his father's sins pressing down on him. This was where it had all begun, where the echoes had been twisted and corrupted, where the malevolent force had been born.

And now, it was where it would end.

The air in the room grew heavy, almost suffocating, as the shadows coalesced into a dark, swirling mass in the center of the room. The mass seemed to pulse with a life of its own, growing larger, more defined, until it took on a vaguely human shape—tall and gaunt, with eyes that burned with an unnatural light.

The force had taken form, manifesting itself in the physical world, and it was more terrifying than any of them could have imagined.

The figure looked at them, its gaze piercing, its presence filling the room with a crushing weight. The echoes swirled around it, feeding it, giving it strength, and as it opened its mouth to speak, the room was filled with a sound that was both a roar and a whisper, a voice that seemed to come from every corner of the asylum.

"Why have you come?" the force hissed, its voice filled with malice. "Why do you seek to destroy what you cannot understand?"

Aaron stepped forward, his heart pounding in his chest, his voice steady. "We've come to end this," he said, his gaze unwavering. "To end the suffering, the pain, the fear. We've come to stop you."

The force laughed, a sound that sent chills down their spines. "You cannot stop me," it said, its voice filled with certainty. "I am the embodiment of your darkest fears, your deepest guilt. I am the echoes of the past, the blood that was spilled on this cursed land. You cannot destroy what is a part of you."

Elena stepped forward, her hand clutching the journal, her voice trembling with emotion. "You're wrong," she said, her gaze fierce. "We can destroy you, because we are not bound by the past. We have the power to break the cycle, to end the curse that you've fed on for so long."

The force's eyes narrowed, its form shifting and writhing as it spoke. "You are nothing but children playing with forces you cannot hope to control. The echoes are mine, bound to me by blood, by the suffering of generations. You are nothing compared to the power I hold."

Aaron looked at Elena, his heart swelling with a mixture of fear and determination. He could feel the weight of his father's sins pressing down on him, the guilt that had haunted him for so long threatening to consume him. But he knew that he couldn't give in to it, that he couldn't let the force win.

He turned back to the figure, his voice strong. "You may be powerful, but you're not invincible. You've fed on our fear, our guilt, but we're not the same people we were when you first took hold of us. We've faced our demons, we've faced the past, and we're not afraid of you anymore."

The force let out a roar, the sound reverberating through the room, shaking the very walls of the asylum. The shadows swirled around them, growing darker, more oppressive, as the figure moved closer, its presence filling the room with a suffocating weight.

Mark and Sarah stood their ground, their faces set with determination, as the force drew closer, its eyes burning with a fierce, unnatural light.

Elena opened the journal, her hands trembling as she read the words of the ritual, the words that her great-grandfather had used to bind the echoes to their bloodline. The words were ancient, written in a language she barely understood, but she knew that they held the key to breaking the curse, to severing the connection between the force and the echoes.

As she spoke the words, the air in the room seemed to shift, the shadows pulling back, the oppressive weight lifting. The force let out a hiss, its form writhing and twisting as the words took hold, weakening its grip on the echoes.

But the force was not ready to be defeated. It lashed out, sending a wave of darkness crashing over them, the shadows pressing in on all sides, suffocating them, drowning them in a sea of fear and guilt.

Aaron felt the darkness closing in around him, the weight of his father's sins pressing down on him like a vice. The memories of the past flooded his mind—his mother's breakdown, his father's experiments, the lives that had been lost because of the darkness his family had unleashed. The guilt was overwhelming, crushing, and for a moment, he felt himself slipping into the abyss, felt the darkness pulling him down.

But then he heard Elena's voice, clear and strong, cutting through the darkness like a beacon of light. She was still speaking the words of the ritual, her voice steady, her resolve unshaken.

And in that moment, Aaron realized that he couldn't let the force win, couldn't let the guilt and fear consume him. He had to face it, had to embrace it, had to accept the past and move forward.

With a surge of determination, Aaron fought back against the darkness, pushing it away, breaking free from its grip. He focused on the light, on the hope that Elena's voice brought him, and slowly, the shadows began to recede, the force's power weakening.

Elena's voice grew stronger, the words of the ritual echoing through the room, the light growing brighter as the force's grip on the echoes loosened. The figure let out a scream, its form writhing and twisting as the light pierced through it, breaking it apart, weakening its hold on the asylum.

Aaron joined Elena, his voice joining hers as they spoke the words of the ritual together, their voices merging into one, their strength growing as they fought back against the darkness.

Mark and Sarah stood beside them, their faces set with determination, their presence lending strength to the ritual, their belief in the power of the light pushing back against the shadows.

The force let out one final, deafening scream, its form shattering, the shadows dissolving into nothingness as the light consumed it. The echoes faded, the voices growing silent, as the malevolent entity that had haunted the asylum for so long was finally destroyed.

The room was filled with a blinding light, the air clear, the oppressive weight lifted. The shadows were gone, the asylum silent, the darkness that had taken root in the land finally banished.

Aaron, Elena, Mark, and Sarah stood together, their breaths coming in ragged gasps, their hearts pounding in their chests. They had done it—they had faced their deepest fears, their darkest guilt, and they had won.

The asylum was still, the walls no longer humming with the weight of the echoes, the air no longer thick with darkness. The ritual had worked—the curse was broken, the force destroyed.

Elena closed the journal, her hands still trembling, but her heart filled with a sense of peace, of closure. She had faced her family's curse, had broken the cycle, and now, she was free.

Aaron looked at her, his eyes filled with gratitude and admiration. "We did it," he said, his voice filled with wonder. "It's over."

Elena smiled, her eyes shining with tears. "Yes," she said, her voice soft. "It's finally over."

Mark and Sarah exchanged a glance, both of them feeling the weight of what they had accomplished, the relief of having survived the final battle, of having faced the darkness and emerged victorious.

As they made their way out of the asylum, the fog had begun to lift, the first light of dawn breaking through the darkness. The sky was a pale, soft blue, the stars fading into the light, and the air was crisp and clear.

They stood together on the steps of the asylum, the building now silent, lifeless, no longer a place of fear and pain, but just an empty shell, a relic of a past that had finally been laid to rest.

Aaron looked at the horizon, the sun beginning to rise, and felt a sense of peace settle over him. The darkness was gone, the echoes silenced, and the weight of his father's sins had been lifted from his shoulders.

Elena took his hand, her touch warm and comforting, and together, they looked out at the dawn, the light of a new day washing over them, filling them with hope for the future.

They had faced the darkness, had confronted their deepest fears, and they had won.

And now, they were free.

Chapter 16: The Gathering Storm

The air in Whistler's Grove was thick with an oppressive weight, as if the very atmosphere had conspired with the malevolent force that loomed over the town. Dark clouds churned in the sky, a tempest brewing on the horizon, and the wind howled through the streets with an eerie, almost mournful wail. The storm was coming, both in the heavens above and in the hearts of those who had been chosen to face the darkness.

Aaron stood by the window of his living room, staring out at the rapidly darkening sky. The first drops of rain had begun to fall, tapping against the glass like skeletal fingers. The storm outside was a perfect reflection of the turmoil within him—chaotic, uncontrollable, and growing stronger by the minute. He clenched his fists, his knuckles turning white as he tried to suppress the rising tide of fear that threatened to overwhelm him.

Behind him, Elena, Mark, and Sarah sat in a tense silence, each of them lost in their own thoughts, their own fears. The room was dimly lit, the flickering light from a single lamp casting long shadows across the walls. The air was thick with the scent of impending rain and something else—something darker, more sinister.

Aaron turned away from the window, his gaze settling on the three people who had become his allies in this battle against the unknown. They looked as worn and frayed as he felt, their faces etched with worry, their eyes haunted by the knowledge of what lay ahead.

"We need to talk," Aaron said, his voice breaking the heavy silence. He walked to the center of the room, standing beside the small coffee table that was cluttered with books, papers, and a map of the town.

"The storm is getting worse, and so is the force. We don't have much time."

Elena nodded, her eyes dark and serious. "I had another vision last night," she said, her voice steady but laced with unease. "It wasn't like the others—it was more fragmented, harder to understand. But I think the storm... it's not just a coincidence. The force is drawing power from it, feeding on the chaos."

Mark leaned forward, his brow furrowed in concern. "The storm is amplifying the force?"

Elena hesitated, then nodded. "Yes. It's like the storm and the force are connected, two parts of the same whole. The echoes... they were stronger in the vision, more vivid. I think the force is using the storm to reach into the town, to spread its influence even further."

Sarah, who had been quietly flipping through an old, leather-bound book, looked up, her expression grave. "That makes sense," she said. "Storms have always been symbols of chaos and destruction. In many cultures, they're seen as harbingers of change, often violent change. If the force is tied to the land, then it would make sense that it could draw power from the storm, using it as a conduit to spread its influence."

Aaron felt a cold knot of fear tighten in his chest. "We need to find a way to stop it, to break its connection to the storm before it's too late."

Sarah nodded, her eyes flicking back to the book in her hands. "I've been doing some research," she said, her voice thoughtful. "There's an ancient ritual that might work, a way to sever the connection between the force and the land. But it's not without risk."

Mark raised an eyebrow. "What kind of risk?"

Sarah hesitated, her fingers tracing the edge of the page. "The ritual requires a significant personal sacrifice. It's not just about offering something up—it's about giving a part of yourself, something irreplaceable. The texts I've found are vague, but they suggest that the person performing the ritual would have to give up a piece of their soul."

The room fell silent, the weight of Sarah's words settling over them like a shroud. Aaron felt a chill run down his spine, the idea of such a sacrifice sending a ripple of fear through him.

"A piece of their soul?" Elena echoed, her voice barely above a whisper. "What does that mean?"

Sarah shook her head, her expression troubled. "I'm not entirely sure. The texts are old, written in a language that's difficult to translate. But the general idea is that the person performing the ritual would be forever changed, their soul altered in some fundamental way. It's a sacrifice that can't be undone."

Mark's jaw tightened, his eyes narrowing as he considered the implications. "And without this ritual, we don't stand a chance of stopping the force?"

Sarah met his gaze, her expression grim. "From what I've read, it's the only way to break the connection between the force and the land. The storm is amplifying its power, making it stronger than ever. If we don't sever that connection, the force will only keep growing, and the storm will continue to fuel it."

Aaron felt a cold sweat break out on the back of his neck. The idea of someone sacrificing a piece of their soul—of losing a part of themselves forever—was terrifying. But as he looked around the room, at the faces of the people he had come to care about, he knew that they couldn't afford to back down now. They were the only ones who could stop the force, the only ones who could save the town from the darkness that was closing in.

"We need to do this," Aaron said, his voice firm. "We don't have a choice."

Elena's eyes met his, her gaze filled with a mixture of fear and determination. "But who... who would perform the ritual?"

The question hung in the air, heavy with unspoken dread. No one wanted to volunteer, but they all knew that someone would have to. The storm outside intensified, the wind howling against the windows, as if the force itself were taunting them, daring them to make the sacrifice.

Aaron's heart pounded in his chest, the weight of the decision pressing down on him. He knew that he had a responsibility, that as the son of the man who had unleashed this darkness, it was his burden to bear. But the thought of giving up a piece of his soul, of losing something so essential to who he was, terrified him in a way he had never experienced before.

"I'll do it," Elena said suddenly, her voice breaking the silence. She stood up, her hands trembling slightly, but her gaze was steady. "This started with my family. The echoes, the curse—it's all tied to the Carters. If someone has to make the sacrifice, it should be me."

Aaron felt a surge of panic at her words. "No, Elena, you don't have to do this. We can find another way."

Elena shook her head, her expression resolute. "There is no other way, Aaron. I've been running from this my whole life, hiding from the echoes, from the truth. But I can't run anymore. If this is the only way to stop the force, then I have to do it."

Mark stood up, his expression hard. "You're not doing this alone, Elena. We'll figure this out together. There has to be a way to perform the ritual without you losing a part of yourself."

Sarah nodded, her gaze softening as she looked at Elena. "We'll find a way to protect you, to minimize the impact of the sacrifice. But we have to be prepared for the worst."

Aaron felt a mixture of relief and dread at their words. He didn't want Elena to go through with the ritual, but he knew that they didn't have much time. The storm was growing stronger by the minute, and with it, the force was becoming more powerful, more dangerous.

He looked out the window, at the storm that was now raging outside, the sky black and furious, the rain coming down in sheets. The storm was a physical manifestation of the chaos within him, within all of them, a reminder of the darkness they were fighting against.

But it was also a reminder of what they stood to lose if they failed.

"We'll do this together," Aaron said, his voice firm. "We'll face the storm, face the force, and we'll find a way to break its hold on this town."

Elena nodded, her eyes filled with determination. "Together."

As they gathered around the table, the storm outside continued to rage, the wind howling like a banshee, the rain lashing against the windows with a ferocity that matched the turmoil in their hearts.

They knew that the battle ahead would be their greatest challenge yet, a test of their strength, their resolve, and their willingness to make the ultimate sacrifice.

But they also knew that they couldn't back down. They couldn't let the darkness win.

The storm was coming, and with it, the final confrontation with the force that had haunted them for so long. But they were ready, ready to face the storm, ready to face their fears, and ready to make the sacrifices necessary to save the town they had come to love.

Because they had to. There was no other choice.

Chapter 17: The Town Under Siege

Whistler's Grove was unrecognizable. The storm had transformed the town into a nightmarish landscape, where the very air seemed charged with a malevolent energy. The sky was a swirling mass of black clouds, punctuated by jagged forks of lightning that illuminated the town in brief, blinding flashes. The wind howled like a chorus of tortured souls, tearing through the streets with a fury that rattled windows and sent debris flying.

Mark Harris drove through the deserted streets, his knuckles white on the steering wheel as he struggled to keep the car steady against the gusts of wind. The police scanner crackled with reports of strange sightings, violent outbursts, and cries for help, but the usual chatter of dispatchers had devolved into static and incoherent voices, as if the storm had reached into the very airwaves to spread its chaos.

He turned a corner, the headlights cutting through the sheets of rain, revealing the once-peaceful neighborhood now shrouded in darkness and fear. Houses that had been filled with warmth and light were now darkened husks, their windows shattered, their doors hanging open like gaping mouths. The streets were empty, but the echoes of past horrors seemed to linger in the air, haunting the town with memories that refused to stay buried.

Mark slowed the car as he approached the town square, where a group of people had gathered, huddled together in the shadow of the old courthouse. They looked like ghosts—pale, trembling, their eyes wide with fear as they clung to one another, desperate for some semblance of safety.

He pulled over and stepped out of the car, the wind nearly knocking him off his feet as he fought his way toward the group. The rain was relentless, soaking him to the bone, but he barely noticed, his focus entirely on the people before him.

"What's happening?" one of the women cried, her voice barely audible over the storm. "What's going on?"

Mark reached out, trying to calm her, but there was a wildness in her eyes that sent a chill down his spine. "It's the storm," he said, though he knew that wasn't the full truth. "You need to get inside, somewhere safe. This isn't going to end anytime soon."

But even as he spoke, Mark knew there was no safe place left in Whistler's Grove. The force was everywhere now, manifesting in ways he couldn't have imagined. As if to prove his point, a loud crash echoed through the square, followed by the sound of breaking glass and a scream that was abruptly cut short.

Mark's heart pounded as he turned toward the source of the noise, his hand instinctively reaching for the gun at his hip. The shadows seemed to writhe and twist, forming shapes that defied logic, and for a brief, terrifying moment, he thought he saw the flicker of red eyes in the darkness.

"We need to move," Mark said, his voice urgent. "Get to the church—it's one of the few buildings that's still intact. Barricade yourselves inside and don't come out until this is over."

The group hesitated, their fear paralyzing them, but another scream, this one closer, spurred them into action. They scattered, running through the rain toward the distant silhouette of the church, their footsteps echoing through the empty streets.

Mark watched them go, a sense of dread settling in his gut. The town was falling apart, the storm tearing at the very fabric of reality, and he knew that the force was behind it all, manipulating the elements, feeding off the collective fear of the townspeople.

As he turned back to his car, the radio crackled to life, a voice cutting through the static. "Chief Harris, this is Officer Jenkins—do you copy?"

Mark grabbed the radio, relief flooding through him at the sound of a familiar voice. "Jenkins, what's your status?"

"We're pinned down near the old mill," Jenkins replied, his voice tense. "There's something out here, Chief—something not human. We've lost two men already, and the others are starting to lose it. We need backup, now."

Mark's blood ran cold. "I'm on my way," he said, starting the car. "Hold your position, and whatever you do, don't engage. We're dealing with something beyond our control."

He threw the car into gear, the tires spinning on the wet pavement as he sped toward the mill. The streets were a blur of rain and shadows, the buildings on either side looming like silent sentinels, watching as the town descended into madness.

As he drove, Mark couldn't shake the feeling that the storm was alive, that it was watching him, waiting for the right moment to strike. The force was using the storm to amplify its power, driving the townspeople to the brink of insanity, and Mark knew that if they didn't stop it soon, Whistler's Grove would be lost.

The mill came into view, its towering silhouette barely visible through the rain. Mark could see the flash of gunfire, the sound of bullets echoing through the storm as the officers fought against something that was more shadow than flesh.

He skidded to a stop, leaping out of the car with his gun drawn. Jenkins and the remaining officers were huddled behind a stack of crates, their faces pale and terrified as they fired blindly into the darkness.

"Chief!" Jenkins called out, relief evident in his voice as Mark crouched beside him. "Thank God you're here. We're getting slaughtered out here—whatever that thing is, it's not human."

Mark peered into the darkness, his heart pounding in his chest. The rain was coming down in sheets, obscuring his vision, but he could see something moving in the shadows—something large and fast, with glowing eyes that seemed to pierce through the storm.

"Hold your fire," Mark ordered, his voice steady despite the fear clawing at his insides. "We're not going to take this thing down with bullets."

The officers hesitated, then slowly lowered their weapons, their eyes wide with fear. The creature in the darkness snarled, the sound low and guttural, sending a shiver down Mark's spine.

He knew that they were outmatched, that this was something beyond their comprehension. The force was using the storm to manifest its power, to twist reality into something dark and nightmarish, and they were caught in the middle of it.

But as he stared into the storm, Mark felt a surge of determination. He had sworn to protect this town, to keep its people safe, and he wasn't going to back down now. Not when they were so close to the end.

"Fall back to the car," Mark said, his voice firm. "We need to regroup with Aaron and the others. They're our best chance at stopping this."

The officers hesitated, then nodded, following Mark as he led them back to the car. The creature snarled again, its glowing eyes tracking their movements, but it didn't follow, as if it were waiting for something—waiting for the storm to fully consume the town.

They piled into the car, Mark gunning the engine as he sped away from the mill, the rain lashing against the windshield like a thousand tiny daggers. The streets were eerily quiet now, the echoes of past atrocities playing out in the distance, ghostly figures flickering in and out of existence as the force bent time and space to its will.

Mark's mind raced as he drove, his thoughts consumed by the madness that had overtaken Whistler's Grove. The force was using the storm to spread its influence, to amplify the echoes of the past, and he knew that they were running out of time.

As they neared Aaron's house, the storm seemed to intensify, the wind howling with a fury that rattled the windows. The sky was a churning mass of black clouds, the lightning illuminating the town in brief, terrifying flashes.

Mark skidded to a stop in front of the house, the officers scrambling out of the car as they made their way to the front door. He could feel the weight of the storm pressing down on him, the force's influence growing stronger with each passing moment.

Inside, Aaron and Sarah were pacing the living room, their faces etched with worry. Elena was sitting on the couch, her eyes closed as she concentrated on the echo that had taken hold of her mind.

Mark stepped inside, shaking the rain from his jacket as he looked around the room. The tension was palpable, the air thick with fear and anticipation.

"We've got a problem," Mark said, his voice grim. "The storm is tearing the town apart. The force is using it to amplify the echoes, to manipulate the people. We've already lost control of most of the town."

Aaron's face darkened, his hands clenching into fists. "We need to act now," he said, his voice filled with determination. "We can't let this continue. The force is growing stronger by the minute."

Elena opened her eyes, her gaze distant and haunted. "I saw it," she whispered, her voice trembling. "I saw the moment the land was cursed. The massacre... the blood that was spilled... it's all connected. The force is rooted in that trauma, in the pain and suffering of the people who died here. It's been feeding off it for centuries, and now it's trying to consume the town."

Sarah's eyes widened, her hand covering her mouth in horror. "The force isn't just targeting individuals—it's targeting the collective trauma of the town. That's why the echoes are so strong, why the storm is amplifying them. It's feeding off the pain of everyone who's ever lived here."

Mark felt a cold knot of fear settle in his gut. The force was more

powerful than they had realized, its roots buried deep in the history of Whistler's Grove. It wasn't just about guilt or fear—it was about the collective trauma of an entire community, a trauma that had festered for generations.

"We have to stop it," Aaron said, his voice firm. "We have to break the cycle, sever the force's connection to the land. If we don't, the town will be lost."

Elena nodded, her expression resolute. "I know what we have to do. The ritual... it's the only way. But we'll need to act quickly, before the storm consumes everything."

Mark looked at each of them in turn, seeing the determination in their eyes. They were all that stood between the town and total destruction, and he knew that they couldn't afford to fail.

"Then let's do this," Mark said, his voice filled with resolve. "For the town, for the people who've suffered... we end this tonight."

The group gathered around the table, their minds racing as they made their final preparations. The storm raged outside, the force's influence growing stronger with each passing moment, but they were ready. Ready to face the darkness, ready to confront the past, and ready to make the sacrifices necessary to save the town.

The battle for Whistler's Grove had begun, and there was no turning back.

Chapter 18: The Bloodline's Burden

The drive to Elena's family home was shrouded in an eerie silence, broken only by the relentless pounding of rain on the windshield and the occasional rumble of thunder that echoed like a distant drumbeat. The storm had grown in intensity, a physical manifestation of the turmoil that roiled within Elena as she sat beside Aaron, her thoughts a chaotic whirl of fear, anger, and determination.

The road was flanked by towering trees, their branches bending under the weight of the wind, as if bowing to the storm's ferocity. The darkness was thick, impenetrable, and the headlights of the car barely made a dent in it, illuminating only the immediate path ahead.

Elena's family home was a relic from another time, a grand, weathered estate that had once stood proudly on the outskirts of Whistler's Grove. Now, it loomed like a ghost from the past, its walls streaked with age, its windows dark and empty. The house was steeped in history, filled with relics from generations past, and the weight of that history pressed down on Elena as they pulled into the long, gravel driveway.

Aaron parked the car, the engine ticking as it cooled in the oppressive air. They sat in silence for a moment, neither of them eager to step out into the storm, neither of them eager to face what lay ahead. But they both knew they had no choice.

"We need to find answers," Aaron said, breaking the silence. His voice was calm, but she could hear the tension beneath it. "Whatever your great-grandfather did, whatever curse he bound to your family—it's the key to stopping the force."

Elena nodded, her throat tight. "I know. But I'm scared, Aaron. Scared of what we'll find… scared of what it means for me."

Aaron reached over, his hand covering hers, his touch warm despite the cold fear that gripped them both. "You're not alone in this, Elena. We'll face it together."

His words were a lifeline, and she clung to them as she opened the car door and stepped out into the storm. The wind whipped her hair around her face, the rain lashing against her skin like needles, but she barely felt it. Her entire focus was on the house before her, on the answers it held within its ancient walls.

The front door creaked ominously as they pushed it open, the sound swallowed by the storm's roar. Inside, the house was dark and musty, the air heavy with the scent of old wood and forgotten memories. The floorboards groaned under their weight as they stepped inside, their footsteps echoing through the empty halls.

Elena led the way, her heart pounding in her chest as they made their way to the study at the back of the house. The room had once belonged to her great-grandfather, Jonathan Carter, the man who had started it all—the man who had bound the echoes to their bloodline, cursing them for generations to come.

The study was untouched, preserved as if her great-grandfather had just stepped out for a moment and would return at any time. The walls were lined with shelves, crammed with books and trinkets, and a large oak desk dominated the center of the room, its surface cluttered with papers, old letters, and a dusty oil lamp.

Elena hesitated at the threshold, a shiver running down her spine. She had always avoided this room, even as a child, sensing that it held secrets too dark and too dangerous to uncover. But now, she had no choice.

Aaron stepped beside her, his presence grounding her, giving her the strength to move forward. Together, they crossed the room and began sifting through the papers on the desk, searching for anything that might give them a clue, anything that might explain the curse that had haunted her family for so long.

It wasn't long before Elena found the journal, buried beneath a stack of old letters. The leather cover was cracked and worn, the pages yellowed with age, but the handwriting was still legible, the ink dark and bold.

"This is it," she whispered, her voice trembling as she opened the journal to the first page. The words leapt out at her, each one a hammer blow to her heart.

"*To my descendants,*" the journal began, "*I have done something unforgivable. In my quest for knowledge, I have delved into forces that no man should ever touch. I have bound our family to the echoes of the past, and in doing so, I have cursed us all.*"

Elena's breath caught in her throat as she read, her eyes scanning the pages, each one detailing the ritual that had tied the echoes to the Carter bloodline. Her great-grandfather had believed that by binding the echoes to his family, he could harness their power, use them to gain insight into the past, into the very fabric of reality. But he had been wrong—terribly wrong.

The ritual had unleashed something far darker than he had anticipated, something that had fed on the trauma of the land, growing stronger with each generation. The echoes had become a curse, a burden that had been passed down from parent to child, each one doomed to suffer the consequences of Jonathan Carter's hubris.

Elena's hands trembled as she turned the pages, her heart sinking with each revelation. The journal detailed the steps of the ritual, the words her great-grandfather had spoken, the symbols he had carved into the earth. But it also hinted at a way to undo it—a counter-ritual that could sever the connection between the echoes and the Carter bloodline, but at a great cost.

She looked up at Aaron, her eyes wide with fear. "This is it," she said, her voice barely above a whisper. "This is how we stop it. But... it's going to require a sacrifice."

Aaron's expression darkened, his jaw tightening. "What kind of sacrifice?"

Elena swallowed hard, her fingers tracing the words on the page. "The counter-ritual requires that I confront the force directly, that I offer something of myself—something irreplaceable. My great-grandfather wasn't clear on what it means, but... it sounds like I'll have to give up a part of my soul."

Aaron's heart clenched at her words, a wave of protectiveness surging through him. "No," he said firmly. "We'll find another way. We can't let you do this."

Elena shook her head, her expression resolute. "There is no other way, Aaron. This is my family's curse—my burden to bear. If I don't do this, the force will continue to grow, and it will consume everything."

Aaron's mind raced, torn between his desire to protect Elena and the knowledge that they were running out of time. The storm outside was a constant reminder of the force's power, a reminder that they couldn't afford to hesitate.

As if sensing his turmoil, Elena reached out, her hand resting on his arm. "You don't have to do this alone, either," she said softly. "We'll face it together."

Aaron's gaze softened, his resolve hardening. "Together," he agreed.

They continued to search the study, and it wasn't long before Aaron found another clue—an old, yellowed letter tucked inside a book on the shelf. The handwriting was familiar, and Aaron's heart skipped a beat as he recognized it.

It was a letter from his father, written in the final days before the experiment that had gone so horribly wrong.

Aaron unfolded the letter, his hands shaking slightly as he read the words, each one filled with a sense of regret, of desperation.

"*Aaron,*" the letter began, "*If you are reading this, then it means I have failed. I have spent my life chasing the echoes, believing that I could control them, that I could use them to unlock the secrets of the mind. But in my arrogance, I have unleashed something far darker, something I can no longer control.*"

Aaron's breath hitched as he continued reading, his father's words striking a chord deep within him. The letter detailed the experiment, the steps his father had taken to try and harness the power of the echoes. But it also revealed something more—a deeper understanding of the force's true nature.

"*The force is not just a manifestation of guilt or fear,*" the letter continued. "*It is a living entity, born from the trauma of the land, from the blood that was spilled here long before the asylum was built. It feeds on pain, on suffering, and it grows stronger with each generation.*"

Aaron's heart pounded in his chest as he reached the final lines of the letter. "*There is only one way to weaken it,*" his father wrote. "*You must sever its connection to the echoes, to the land. The ritual I have included may be the only way to do this, but it will require strength, courage, and the willingness to sacrifice everything.*"

Aaron's hands shook as he lowered the letter, the weight of his father's words pressing down on him. The ritual his father had outlined was similar to the one described in Jonathan Carter's journal, but with a key difference—it required the combined knowledge and power of both the Blake and Carter bloodlines.

"We have to do this," Aaron said, his voice filled with determination. "We have to combine the rituals, use the knowledge from both our families to stop the force. It's the only way."

Elena nodded, her expression resolute. "But we'll need to act quickly. The storm is getting worse, and the force is growing stronger. We have to perform the ritual at the height of the storm, when the force is at its most vulnerable."

Aaron looked at her, his heart swelling with a mixture of fear and admiration. "Are you ready for this?"

Elena's gaze met his, and he could see the fear in her eyes, but also the determination, the strength that had been growing within her. "I'm ready," she said, her voice steady. "But we'll do it together."

Aaron reached out, taking her hand in his, the bond between them deepening in that moment. They were bound by more than just the force—they were bound by the choices their ancestors had made, by the responsibility they now carried to right those wrongs.

"We'll end this," Aaron said, his voice filled with conviction. "No matter what it takes."

As they left the study, the storm outside raged on, the wind howling through the trees, the rain lashing against the windows. But inside, there was a sense of calm, a sense of purpose. They had found the answers they needed, and they were ready to face the final battle.

Together, they would confront the darkness, confront the past, and finally break the curse that had haunted their families for so long.

Because they had to. There was no other choice.

Chapter 19: The Weight of the Past

The storm howled around the asylum, a relentless force of nature that seemed to pulse in time with the malevolent energy emanating from the ancient building. The sky was a roiling cauldron of black clouds, split by jagged forks of lightning that illuminated the twisted architecture of the asylum in brief, terrifying flashes. The rain fell in sheets, drenching Aaron, Elena, Mark, and Sarah as they stood before the massive, decaying structure, each of them feeling the oppressive weight of the moment.

Aaron's heart pounded in his chest as he stared at the asylum, his mind racing with the knowledge of what lay ahead. The storm was at its peak, the force inside the asylum growing stronger with each passing second, feeding off the chaos and fear that had gripped Whistler's Grove. The echoes of the past were no longer distant whispers—they were a cacophony, a chorus of pain and suffering that filled the air, pressing down on Aaron like a physical weight.

He knew what they had to do. The ritual they had uncovered, the one that tied the Blake and Carter bloodlines together, was their only chance to sever the connection between the force and the echoes, to break the curse that had plagued their families for generations. But as they approached the asylum, Aaron couldn't shake the feeling that there was something more—something buried deep within his own mind, something that had been hidden from him for years.

The front doors of the asylum creaked open with a sound that sent chills down their spines, and they stepped inside, the darkness swallowing them whole. The interior of the building was just as Aaron remembered—dark, oppressive, filled with the lingering scent of decay and something far darker. The walls were covered in strange symbols, carved into the stone with a precision that spoke of ancient, forbidden knowledge. The air was thick with the echoes, the voices of the past swirling around them, growing louder with each step they took.

Aaron's breath came in shallow gasps as they moved deeper into the asylum, the memories of his childhood—memories he had tried so hard to forget—beginning to resurface. He could feel the walls closing in around him, the weight of the past pressing down on him, suffocating him.

"Are you okay?" Elena's voice cut through the darkness, filled with concern. She reached out, her hand warm on his arm, grounding him in the present.

Aaron forced himself to nod, though his mind was in turmoil. "I'm fine," he said, though the words felt hollow, a lie told more to himself than to her. He wasn't fine—not even close. The asylum was more than just a building—it was a tomb, filled with the ghosts of his past, the secrets he had buried deep within his mind.

They reached the heart of the asylum, a massive chamber at the center of the building, where the walls were covered in more of the strange symbols, their meaning lost to time. The air was thick with the echoes, the voices of the past overlapping, merging into a single, overwhelming roar that made Aaron's head spin.

But it wasn't just the echoes that filled the room—it was something else, something darker. The force was here, a presence that pulsed with malevolent energy, watching them, waiting for the moment to strike.

Aaron felt a cold sweat break out on the back of his neck as he stared at the center of the room, where a large stone altar stood, its surface etched with symbols that matched those on the walls. The altar was the focal point of the force, the place where his father had conducted his final experiment, the experiment that had gone so horribly wrong.

Aaron's heart pounded in his chest as he stepped closer to the altar, the memories of that day—the day his father had died—beginning to surface, each one more painful than the last.

He had been just a boy, no more than ten years old, but the memories were vivid, burned into his mind like a brand. He remembered the fear, the confusion, as his father had brought him to the asylum, insisting that he would understand everything soon, that he was special, that he had a role to play.

Aaron's breath hitched as the memories flooded back, the events of that day playing out in his mind like a film reel that had been stuck on pause for years. His father had been obsessed, driven by a desire to unlock the secrets of the echoes, to harness their power for his own ends. But he hadn't realized the danger—the darkness that lurked beneath the surface, waiting to consume them all.

Aaron remembered the altar, remembered his father standing before it, chanting words in a language Aaron didn't understand, his voice filled with a mixture of fear and desperation. He remembered the symbols on the walls, the way they seemed to pulse with a life of their own, growing brighter with each word his father spoke.

And then he remembered the moment it all went wrong.

Aaron's hands shook as the memory came rushing back, clear and sharp, as if it had happened just moments ago. He had been standing beside the altar, watching his father, trying to understand what was happening, trying to make sense of the chaos that had engulfed them.

But then something had changed—something in the air, something in the way the symbols glowed, as if they were reacting to his presence. Aaron had felt a strange pull, a compulsion to reach out, to touch the altar, to become a part of whatever his father was doing.

And so he had.

Aaron's breath caught in his throat as the memory hit him like a physical blow. He had reached out, his hand brushing against the altar, and in that moment, everything had changed. The symbols had flared with blinding light, the air had crackled with energy, and the force—dark and malevolent—had surged into the room, drawn to Aaron like a moth to a flame.

His father had realized too late what was happening, had tried to stop it, but the force was too strong. It had taken hold of Aaron, used him as a conduit, feeding off his fear, his confusion, his innocence. The echoes had erupted around them, the voices of the past merging into a single, overwhelming roar, and Aaron had screamed, the sound echoing through the chamber, filled with terror and pain.

And then his father had died.

Aaron's legs buckled, and he fell to his knees before the altar, the weight of the memory crushing him. He had killed his father. Not intentionally, not maliciously, but it didn't matter. The force had used him, had fed off him, and his father had paid the price.

"Aaron!" Elena's voice was filled with panic as she dropped to her knees beside him, her hands gripping his shoulders, shaking him. "Aaron, what's wrong?"

Aaron couldn't speak, couldn't breathe. The memory was too much, too overwhelming. The guilt that he had buried deep within him for so many years was now bubbling to the surface, threatening to drown him in its depths.

"I... I killed him," Aaron choked out, his voice barely above a whisper. "I didn't mean to, but I... I killed him."

Elena's eyes widened in shock, her grip on him tightening. "No, Aaron, it wasn't your fault. You were just a child—you couldn't have known."

But Aaron shook his head, the tears streaming down his face. "It was me. The force... it used me. I didn't know what I was doing, but it used me to get to him. And now... now it's using all of us."

Elena's heart broke for him, but she knew that this moment—this painful, agonizing moment—was necessary. Aaron had to confront his past, had to confront the truth about what had happened if they were going to stand any chance of defeating the force.

"Aaron," she said softly, her voice filled with compassion, "you didn't kill your father. The force did. It manipulated you, used you because it knew you were vulnerable. But that doesn't mean it was your fault."

Aaron looked up at her, his eyes filled with pain. "But I can't... I can't stop thinking about it. The memory... it's like it's been locked away all these years, and now it's come back, and it's too much. It's too much, Elena."

Elena nodded, understanding the depth of his pain. "I know it feels like that now, but you're stronger than you think, Aaron. You've carried this guilt for so long, and it's time to let it go. It's time to face it, to accept what happened, and to use that knowledge to fight back against the force."

Aaron's breath hitched as her words sank in. She was right—he had to let go of the guilt, had to accept what had happened, or the force would continue to feed off his pain, off his fear. It would continue to manipulate him, just as it had done all those years ago.

But letting go wasn't easy. The memory was a part of him, a scar that had shaped his entire life, and the thought of releasing it, of forgiving himself, felt impossible.

"I don't know if I can do it," he admitted, his voice trembling.

Elena's gaze softened, and she cupped his face in her hands, her touch gentle, reassuring. "You can, Aaron. I'm here with you. We'll do it together."

Aaron took a deep, shuddering breath, his mind racing, the memories swirling around him, threatening to pull him under. But he focused on Elena, on her words, on her presence, and slowly, the panic began to recede.

He had to do this. He had to confront the truth, had to face the memory

, and he had to let it go. If he didn't, the force would win, and everything they had fought for, everything they had sacrificed, would be for nothing.

Aaron closed his eyes, forcing himself to relive the memory one last time. He saw his father, standing before the altar, his face twisted with fear, with desperation. He saw the symbols glowing, saw his own hand reaching out, saw the light flaring as the force surged into the room.

And then he saw his father's death—saw the way the life had drained from his eyes, saw the way his body had crumpled to the ground, lifeless, empty.

It wasn't your fault.

The words echoed in his mind, a mantra that he clung to as the memory played out, over and over. It wasn't your fault. It wasn't your fault.

The guilt that had weighed on him for so long began to lift, the heavy chains of self-blame slowly falling away. He had been a child, innocent, unknowing, and the force had taken advantage of that. It had used him, manipulated him, and in the process, it had destroyed his father.

But that didn't mean it was his fault.

With each repetition of the memory, the pain lessened, the sharp edges of the guilt dulling, until all that was left was a deep, aching sadness. But it was a sadness he could live with, a sadness that he could bear.

When Aaron finally opened his eyes, he felt lighter, freer. The memory was still there, but it no longer held the power it once had. It was a part of him, yes, but it didn't define him.

"I'm ready," Aaron said quietly, his voice steady, resolute. "Let's finish this."

Elena smiled, her eyes shining with pride. "Together," she said, her voice filled with determination.

Aaron nodded, rising to his feet, the weight of the past finally lifted from his shoulders. The force was still there, still powerful, but it no longer had a hold on him. He had faced his past, faced the truth, and now he was ready to fight back.

They turned to the altar, the symbols glowing softly in the dim light, the air around them thick with anticipation. The ritual they had uncovered, the one that would sever the connection between the force and the echoes, was their only chance, and they were ready to perform it.

Aaron and Elena stood side by side, their hands intertwined, their hearts beating as one. They had faced the darkness, faced their fears, and now they were ready to take the final step.

As they began the ritual, the storm outside reached its peak, the wind howling, the rain lashing against the walls of the asylum with a fury that matched their own. The echoes swirled around them, the voices of the past merging into a single, powerful chant, as if the very fabric of time was bending to their will.

Aaron closed his eyes, focusing on the words of the ritual, on the power that flowed through him, through Elena, through the bloodlines that had been bound together for so long. He could feel the force resisting, fighting back with everything it had, but he didn't waver. He had accepted his past, had accepted his guilt, and now he was ready to let it all go.

The symbols on the altar flared with light, the air crackling with energy, and Aaron felt the force begin to weaken, its grip on the echoes loosening. The power that had once seemed so overwhelming, so unstoppable, was now faltering, crumbling under the weight of the truth, under the weight of their resolve.

As the final words of the ritual echoed through the chamber, Aaron felt a surge of energy, a surge of power that filled him with a sense of peace, of closure. The force was gone, its connection to the echoes severed, its power finally broken.

Aaron opened his eyes, his breath coming in slow, steady gasps, his heart pounding in his chest. The chamber was silent, the storm outside beginning to recede, the echoes finally at rest.

He looked at Elena, his heart swelling with gratitude, with love. They had done it. They had faced the darkness, faced the past, and they had won.

Chapter 20: The Aftermath

The storm had passed, leaving the world in a state of eerie calm. The first light of dawn broke over the horizon, painting the sky in soft hues of pink and orange, a stark contrast to the darkness that had consumed Whistler's Grove just hours before. The air was fresh and cool, the scent of rain lingering, and the oppressive weight that had hung over the town for so long was finally lifting.

The asylum lay in ruins, its once-imposing structure now a crumbling shell of what it had been. The walls were cracked and broken, the windows shattered, and the strange symbols that had once pulsed with dark energy were now faded, their power gone. The echoes, those haunting voices from the past, had dissipated with the force's defeat, leaving behind only silence.

Aaron stood at the edge of the asylum's grounds, his eyes fixed on the horizon as the sun began to rise. The weight of the night's events still pressed down on him, but it was a different kind of weight—a quieter, more bearable burden. The guilt that had once consumed him, that had shaped his every thought and action, was no longer the dominant force in his life. He had faced his past, confronted the truth, and in doing so, had found a measure of peace.

Beside him, Elena stood silently, her gaze also on the horizon. Her face was pale, her eyes tired, but there was a quiet strength in her posture, a sense of resolve that had not been there before. She had accepted her role in the events that had unfolded, had taken on the burden of her family's curse, and had emerged stronger for it.

The wind stirred the leaves around them, carrying with it the faint scent of earth and rain. It was a new day, a day without the dark presence of the force, a day where the echoes were finally at rest.

Mark and Sarah approached from the ruins of the asylum, their footsteps slow and deliberate, as if they were each carrying the weight of a thousand memories. Mark's face was lined with exhaustion, but his eyes were clear, focused. He had fulfilled his duty to the town, had protected it from the darkness, and in doing so, had come to terms with the legacy of his family. The burden of his father's past had been heavy, but Mark had carried it with honor, and now, as the sun rose, he felt a sense of release, of closure.

Sarah, too, bore the signs of the night's ordeal. Her usual calm demeanor had been replaced by a quiet introspection, her thoughts turned inward as she processed the events that had unfolded. She had seen things she could never have imagined, had faced the supernatural in a way that had shattered her previous beliefs. But in the process, she had also found a new sense of purpose, a new understanding of the complexities of the human mind and the forces that could influence it.

The four of them stood together in the early morning light, each lost in their own thoughts, each processing the trauma of the night in their own way. The silence was comforting, a space where they could begin to heal, to recover from the wounds—both physical and psychological—that had been inflicted upon them.

Aaron finally broke the silence, his voice low, reflective. "It's over," he said, the words carrying a weight of finality. "The force is gone, the echoes... they're at peace."

Elena nodded, her gaze still on the horizon. "But the scars remain," she said quietly. "Not just on us, but on the town, on the people who lived through this."

Mark sighed, running a hand through his hair. "Whistler's Grove has seen its share of darkness," he said, his voice tinged with sadness. "But it's a resilient place. The people here... they'll recover, in time."

"But they'll never forget," Sarah added, her tone thoughtful. "Trauma like this... it leaves a mark, even if the immediate danger is gone. The memories, the fear—it lingers, sometimes just beneath the surface."

Aaron glanced at her, understanding the truth of her words. He knew all too well how trauma could fester, how it could shape a person's life, influence their actions, their thoughts. But he also knew that there was a way forward, a path to healing, if one was willing to take the first step.

"We'll all need time," Aaron said, his voice firm but gentle. "Time to process what's happened, to understand it, and to find a way to move on. But we can't do it alone. We'll need to support each other, to be there for each other, just as we were last night."

Elena looked at him, her eyes filled with a mixture of gratitude and resolve. "We'll need to help the town too," she said. "The people here... they've been through so much. We can't just leave them to deal with this on their own."

Mark nodded in agreement. "We'll stay," he said, his voice carrying a note of determination. "We'll help them rebuild, help them heal. Whistler's Grove is our home, and we're not going to abandon it now."

Sarah smiled softly, a sense of calm settling over her. "I think we've all learned something about ourselves," she said. "About what we're capable of, about our strengths and our weaknesses. But more than that, we've learned the importance of facing our fears, of not letting the past define us."

Aaron's gaze shifted back to the horizon, the sun now fully risen, casting its warm light over the landscape. The darkness that had once seemed so impenetrable, so all-consuming, was now receding, replaced by the soft glow of a new day.

"We've all been through our own hell," Aaron said quietly. "But we've come out the other side. We've faced the darkness, and we've survived. And now... now it's time to start living again."

Elena reached out, taking his hand in hers, the gesture simple but filled with meaning. "Together," she said, echoing the word they had spoken to each other so many times in the last few days. "We'll do it together."

Aaron squeezed her hand, the bond between them stronger than ever. They had been through so much, had faced the very worst that the world could throw at them, and they had emerged victorious. But the victory was not just in defeating the force—it was in the growth, the understanding, the acceptance that had come from the journey.

Mark and Sarah stepped closer, the four of them standing together, a small but determined group, united by their experiences, by the trauma they had faced, and by the knowledge that they were stronger together than they had ever been alone.

The asylum, now a ruin, stood as a testament to the past, to the horrors that had once been contained within its walls. But it was also a symbol of the resilience of the human spirit, of the ability to confront darkness, to face trauma, and to come out the other side with a renewed sense of purpose.

As the sun continued to rise, casting its golden light over the ruins, the group began to move, slowly making their way back to the town. There was work to be done, people to help, and lives to rebuild. But they were ready for it, ready to face whatever challenges lay ahead, because they knew that they had already faced the worst, and they had survived.

Aaron walked beside Elena, his hand still in hers, feeling a sense of peace that he hadn't felt in years. The memories of the past, the trauma that had once defined him, were still there, but they no longer held the power they once had. He had confronted his guilt, had accepted the truth, and in doing so, had found a way to move forward.

Elena, too, had found a new sense of purpose, a new understanding of her role in the world. The curse that had haunted her family for generations was broken, and with it, the weight of responsibility that had been placed on her shoulders. But instead of feeling lost, she felt empowered, ready to take on whatever came next.

Mark and Sarah walked a few steps behind them, their own thoughts focused on the future. Mark had found a way to reconcile the past, to accept the legacy of his family, and to forge a new path forward. Sarah had faced her fears, had seen the supernatural with her own eyes, and had come to a new understanding of the world, one that was both terrifying and exhilarating.

As they reached the edge of the asylum's grounds, they paused, turning back to look at the ruins one last time. The building that had once been a place of horror, of darkness, was now just a shell, a remnant of a past that no longer had a hold on them.

"It's over," Aaron said, his voice filled with a quiet satisfaction. "We've done what we came to do."

Elena nodded, a small smile on her lips. "Yes, we have. And now... now it's time to look to the future."

The group turned away from the asylum, walking toward the town, the dawn breaking fully over the landscape, bringing with it the promise of a new day, a new beginning.

They had faced the darkness, had confronted their fears, and had emerged stronger for it. And as they walked together, side by side, they knew that whatever the future held, they would face it together, with the strength and the courage that had brought them through the storm.

The past was behind them, the trauma processed, the wounds beginning to heal. And as the sun rose higher in the sky, casting its light over Whistler's Grove, they knew that the worst was over, and the best was yet to come.

Chapter 21: Elena's New Beginning

The morning light streamed through the windows of Elena's apartment, casting warm, golden beams across the floor and filling the space with a serene glow. The room, once cluttered and chaotic, was now a sanctuary of calm and order. The walls, which had once been adorned with dark, disturbing drawings, now displayed art that reflected a sense of hope and renewal—landscapes bathed in light, peaceful scenes of nature, and abstract forms that spoke of transformation and growth.

Elena stood in the center of the room, taking it all in, a small smile playing on her lips. The apartment felt different now, almost as if it had undergone a transformation as profound as her own. The echoes that had once tormented her were gone, their dark whispers replaced by the gentle hum of morning activity outside her window—the distant sound of birdsong, the rustle of leaves in the breeze, the muffled laughter of children playing in the street.

She moved to the window, her hand resting on the cool glass as she looked out at Whistler's Grove, the town that had been both a source of pain and a place of healing. The storm had passed, and with it, the darkness that had haunted the town for so long. The streets were calm, the buildings standing tall and proud, and there was a sense of normalcy returning to the community, a collective sigh of relief as life began to move forward once more.

But Elena knew that the scars of the past still lingered, hidden beneath the surface. The events that had unfolded over the past days had left their mark on the town, on its people, and on her. Yet, instead of feeling burdened by the weight of those experiences, Elena felt something new—something powerful and affirming. She felt a sense of purpose, of resolve, a calling that she could no longer ignore.

She had spent so long running from her past, from the echoes, from the darkness that had been passed down through her family. But now, she saw it all in a different light. The echoes had been a curse, yes, but they had also been a gift—a gift that had allowed her to see into the hearts and minds of others, to understand their pain, their fears, their traumas. And now, she was ready to use that gift to help others, to guide them through their own darkness and into the light.

Elena turned away from the window, her gaze falling on the desk in the corner of the room. It was neatly organized, the surface clear except for a few books and a notebook she had begun to fill with her thoughts, her plans for the future. She walked over to it, her fingers brushing over the pages as she flipped through the notebook, her mind racing with ideas.

She had decided to stay in Whistler's Grove. It was a decision that had come to her in the quiet moments after the storm had passed, as she had sat in the ruins of the asylum, reflecting on everything that had happened. The town needed healing, just as she had, and she wanted to be a part of that process. She wanted to help others who had been affected by the echoes, by the force, by the trauma that had been unearthed.

Elena's thoughts turned to the people she had met over the past days—Aaron, Mark, Sarah. They had all been through so much, had faced their own demons, and had emerged stronger for it. They had become more than just allies in a battle against the supernatural; they had become friends, bound by their shared experiences, their shared pain. And now, they were all moving forward, each in their own way, each finding a new path in the aftermath of the storm.

For Elena, that path led to a new role, one she had never imagined for herself but now embraced fully. She would become a protector, a guide for those who were lost in their own darkness, who were struggling with their own echoes. She would help them find their way out, just as she had found hers.

She had already begun to take steps in that direction, reaching out to the people of Whistler's Grove, offering her support, her understanding. She had spoken with Aaron about the possibility of setting up a center in the town, a place where people could come to talk, to heal, to learn how to live with the memories that haunted them. Aaron had been supportive, offering his expertise as a psychiatrist, and together, they had begun to lay the groundwork for what would become a haven for those in need.

Elena sat down at the desk, her pen in hand as she began to write, her thoughts flowing onto the page. She wrote about the importance of healing, of processing trauma, of not letting the past define the future. She wrote about the therapeutic techniques she had learned from Aaron, from Sarah—cognitive behavioral therapy, mindfulness, grounding exercises—all tools that could help people regain control over their lives, tools that she would use in her new role.

As she wrote, she reflected on her own journey, on the transformation she had undergone. She had started as a victim, plagued by the echoes, tormented by the darkness that had followed her for so long. But through it all, she had found strength, resilience, a determination to survive, to fight back. She had faced her fears, had confronted the truth about her family's past, and had emerged stronger, more certain of who she was and what she was meant to do.

Elena paused, her pen hovering over the page as she thought about the people she would help, the lives she would touch. She knew that the road ahead would not be easy, that there would be setbacks, challenges, moments of doubt. But she also knew that she was not alone, that she had the support of her friends, her new family, and that together, they could create something beautiful out of the darkness.

The sound of a knock on the door pulled her from her thoughts, and she set the pen down, standing up to answer it. As she opened the door, she was greeted by the familiar faces of Aaron, Mark, and Sarah, their expressions warm and welcoming.

"We thought we'd check in on you," Aaron said, a smile tugging at the corners of his lips. "See how you're doing."

Elena smiled back, stepping aside to let them in. "I'm doing well," she said, and she meant it. "Just thinking about what's next."

Mark glanced around the apartment, noting the changes. "Looks like you've already started," he said, his tone approving. "The place looks great."

"Thanks," Elena said, closing the door behind them. "I've been thinking a lot about the future, about how I can help the people here. There's so much work to be done, but I'm ready for it."

Sarah nodded, her gaze thoughtful. "You've come a long way, Elena," she said softly. "We all have. But I think you're going to make a real difference here. The town needs someone like you, someone who understands what they're going through."

Elena felt a warmth spread through her at Sarah's words, a sense of validation that she hadn't realized she needed. "I hope so," she said, her voice filled with quiet determination. "I've seen what trauma can do, how it can shape a person's life. But I also know that healing is possible, that there's a way forward."

Aaron stepped closer, his eyes meeting hers. "You're not alone in this," he said. "We're all here to support you, to help you in any way we can. We're in this together."

Elena nodded, feeling the truth of his words deep in her heart. They had faced the darkness together, had survived the storm, and now they were united in their commitment to healing, to rebuilding, to creating a future that was brighter, more hopeful.

The four of them sat down in the living room, the conversation flowing easily as they talked about their plans, their hopes for the future. They discussed the center they were going to establish, the programs they would offer, the ways they would reach out to the community. It was a conversation filled with optimism, with a sense of purpose that had been hard-won through their shared experiences.

As the morning sun continued to rise, filling the apartment with light, Elena felt a deep sense of peace settle over her. She had found her place, her purpose, and she was ready to embrace it fully. The journey that had brought her here had been long, difficult, and filled with pain, but it had also been a journey of growth, of transformation.

She had started as a victim, but now she was a protector, a guide for those who needed help finding their way out of the darkness. And she knew that with the support of her friends, her new family, she could make a difference, could help others heal, just as she had.

The echoes were gone, the force defeated, but the memories would remain. And that was okay. Because Elena had learned that it wasn't about erasing the past—it was about accepting it, understanding it, and using that understanding to move forward.

Elena looked around the room at the faces of her friends, her heart swelling with gratitude, with love. They had been through so much together, had faced their worst fears, and had come out stronger for it. And now, as they sat together in the warmth of the morning sun, she knew that they were ready for whatever the future held.

Together, they would continue to heal, to grow, to rebuild. They would help others who were struggling, who were lost in their own darkness, and they would show them that there was a way out, a way forward.

Because they had faced the darkness, and they had found the light.

And now, they were ready to share that light with the world.

Chapter 22: Mark's Decision

The police station in Whistler's Grove had always been a place of quiet, steadfast order, a bulwark against the chaos that occasionally brushed against the edges of town life. But after the events of the past days, it had taken on a new character—more solemn, more resolute. The storm had passed, the immediate danger had been vanquished, but the echoes of what had transpired lingered in the minds of those who had survived. The building now felt like the last outpost of sanity in a town that had seen its share of madness.

Mark Harris sat at his desk, the morning sun casting long shadows through the blinds. The once bustling station was eerily still, the usual sounds of ringing phones, shuffling papers, and low conversations replaced by a heavy, contemplative silence. The officers who remained were subdued, each grappling with their own thoughts, their own memories of the storm that had nearly consumed them all.

Mark himself was deep in thought, his mind turning over the events of the past days like a stone he couldn't quite set down. The storm, the malevolent force, the echoes—everything had changed him, had forced him to confront not just the darkness in the town, but the shadows that lurked within himself. He had seen things he could barely comprehend, had faced down horrors that defied logic, and yet, here he was, still standing, still breathing.

But he was different now. The man who had walked into that storm was not the same man who sat at this desk today.

Mark's office was a small, unassuming room, its walls lined with framed photographs of past achievements, commendations for service, and old black-and-white snapshots of the town's earlier days. The desk was cluttered with reports, case files, and a coffee mug that had long gone cold. But the object that held Mark's attention was an old, weathered photograph that sat in a simple wooden frame on the corner of his desk.

It was a photograph of his father, taken when Mark was just a boy. His father had been a police officer too, a man of integrity and strength, someone Mark had always looked up to, even when their relationship had become strained in later years. The image was grainy, a relic from a time before digital cameras, but the pride in his father's eyes was unmistakable. It was a pride that Mark had always strived to live up to, even after his father's death—a death that Mark now knew was tied to the very force they had just defeated.

The weight of that knowledge sat heavily on Mark's shoulders. His father had been caught up in the dark history of Whistler's Grove, a history that Mark had only recently begun to unravel. The secrets his father had kept, the dangers he had faced—all of it had come crashing down on Mark in the midst of the storm. And now, Mark was left to pick up the pieces, to decide what kind of legacy he would leave behind.

He had spent the night poring over old case files, digging through records that had been long forgotten. He had wanted to understand—truly understand—what had happened to his father, what had led him down the path that had ultimately ended in tragedy. The answers were buried in those files, in the town's dark history, in the secrets that had been passed down through generations.

But understanding was not the same as acceptance. Mark had come to realize that some things could never be fully understood, that some mysteries were meant to remain unsolved. What mattered now was how he chose to move forward, how he chose to honor his father's memory while forging his own path.

As he sat in the quiet of his office, Mark felt a renewed sense of purpose beginning to take root within him. The town of Whistler's Grove had been through hell, but it had survived. And now, it needed someone to watch over it, someone to protect it from the darkness that still lurked in the shadows. It needed a guardian.

Mark had always been a protector—of the town, of its people—but now, that role took on a deeper meaning. He understood that Whistler's Grove was a place with a dark history, a history that would never fully go away. The echoes of the past were always there, just beneath the surface, waiting for the right moment to resurface. And while the immediate threat had been vanquished, Mark knew that it was only a matter of time before something else emerged from the shadows.

He couldn't leave. He couldn't turn his back on the town that had shaped him, the town that his father had given his life to protect. No, Mark was more determined than ever to stay, to watch over Whistler's Grove, to ensure that the darkness that had nearly consumed it would never take hold again.

His thoughts were interrupted by a knock on the door. Mark looked up to see Aaron standing in the doorway, his expression calm but thoughtful. Aaron had been through his own transformation, had faced his own demons, and had emerged with a clarity of purpose that Mark both admired and respected.

"Mind if I come in?" Aaron asked, his voice quiet.

Mark nodded, gesturing to the chair across from his desk. "Of course. Have a seat."

Aaron closed the door behind him and sat down, his gaze briefly drifting to the photograph of Mark's father before returning to Mark's face. There was a moment of silence between them, the weight of unspoken words hanging in the air.

"How are you holding up?" Aaron asked, his tone genuine.

Mark sighed, leaning back in his chair. "I've been better," he admitted. "But I've also been worse. I'm still trying to wrap my head around everything that's happened."

Aaron nodded, understanding. "It's a lot to process. We've all been through something that most people couldn't even imagine. But we're still here, and that means something."

Mark glanced at the photograph on his desk, then back at Aaron. "I've been thinking about my father," he said, his voice low. "About the choices he made, the secrets he kept. I always knew there was something he wasn't telling me, something that weighed on him. But I never imagined it would be connected to... all of this."

Aaron listened, his expression thoughtful. "Your father was a good man, Mark. He did what he thought was right, even if it meant keeping those secrets. But you're not him. You have the chance to forge your own path, to make your own choices."

Mark nodded slowly, the truth of Aaron's words settling over him like a blanket of comfort. "I know," he said. "And that's why I've decided to stay. This town... it needs someone to watch over it, someone who understands what's really out there. I've spent my whole life trying to protect this place, and I'm not about to stop now."

Aaron's expression softened, a small smile playing on his lips. "I'm glad to hear that. Whistler's Grove needs you, Mark. We all do."

Mark felt a surge of determination, of purpose. "I've been thinking about what comes next," he said. "About how we can keep an eye on things, make sure that the echoes don't return, that the force doesn't find a way back in. I don't want to just react to these things—I want to prevent them."

Aaron leaned forward, his interest piqued. "What do you have in mind?"

Mark reached for a folder on his desk, sliding it across to Aaron. "I've been putting together a plan," he explained. "A way for us to monitor the town, to stay ahead of any potential threats. We'll need to work together—me, you, Elena, and Sarah. We each have our strengths, our unique perspectives. If we pool our resources, our knowledge, we can make sure that Whistler's Grove stays safe."

Aaron opened the folder, scanning the contents with a thoughtful expression. Inside were detailed notes, maps of the town, and a list of potential vulnerabilities—places where the echoes might reemerge, where the force could potentially gain a foothold.

"This is impressive, Mark," Aaron said, looking up. "You've really thought this through."

Mark nodded. "I have. Because I don't want anyone else to go through what we did. I don't want anyone else to suffer because we weren't prepared."

Aaron closed the folder, a look of determination in his eyes. "Then let's do it," he said. "We'll set up a network, keep an eye on things, and be ready for whatever comes next."

Mark felt a sense of relief, of affirmation. He had made the right choice. Staying in Whistler's Grove, taking on the role of its guardian—it was where he was meant to be. And with Aaron, Elena, and Sarah by his side, he knew they could handle whatever the future might throw at them.

"Thank you, Aaron," Mark said, his voice filled with sincerity. "For everything."

Aaron shook his head, a smile on his face. "We're in this together, Mark. We've all been given a second chance, a chance to make things right. Let's make sure we don't waste it."

Mark nodded, the weight on his shoulders feeling a little lighter. He had found his purpose, his place in the world, and he was ready to embrace it fully.

As Aaron stood to leave, Mark looked around his office, at the photographs on the walls, at the memories that filled the room. This was his home, his community, and he would do everything in his power to protect it.

Aaron paused at the door, turning back to Mark. "We're meeting at Elena's later," he said. "To talk about the center we're setting up. I think you'll want to be a part of that."

Mark smiled, feeling a sense of belonging, of being part of something bigger than himself. "I'll be there," he said.

As Aaron left the office, Mark took a deep breath, letting the air fill his lungs, grounding him in the present. The storm was over, the force was defeated, but the work was just beginning. And Mark was ready for it.

He reached for the folder on his desk, flipping it open once more, his mind already racing with ideas, with plans. There was so much to do, so many ways to protect the town, to ensure that the darkness never returned. But he was up to the task. He had the support of his friends, the strength of his resolve, and the legacy of his father guiding him.

Mark Harris was a guardian now, in every sense of the word. And as he looked out the window, at the peaceful streets of Whistler's Grove, he felt a deep sense of peace, of fulfillment. This was where he was meant to be, where he could make a difference, where he could honor his father's memory by protecting the town he loved.

The darkness had been pushed back, the echoes silenced, but Mark knew that the battle was never truly over. There would always be shadows, always be threats lurking just out of sight. But he was ready for them, ready to stand guard, to watch over Whistler's Grove and its people.

Because this was his town, his community, and he would protect it with everything he had.

Chapter 23: A New Echo, Old Tricks

The late afternoon sun bathed the quiet neighborhood of Whistler's Grove in a warm, golden light. The storm that had ravaged the town was now a distant memory, its fury replaced by a peaceful stillness that seemed almost too perfect, too serene. The air was crisp, carrying the faint scent of blooming flowers and freshly cut grass, and the streets were lined with the comforting sights of everyday life—children playing, neighbors chatting, and families sitting on their porches, enjoying the calm.

But beneath the surface, there was an undercurrent, a subtle tension that only those who had lived through the recent horrors could feel. It was a tension that hung in the air, unseen but palpable, a reminder that the past was never truly gone, that it lingered in the shadows, waiting for the right moment to reassert itself.

In one of the houses on Elm Street, a young boy named Tommy sat on the floor of his bedroom, surrounded by toys and books. He was eight years old, with a mop of unruly brown hair and wide, curious eyes that seemed to take in everything around him. His room was a haven of childhood innocence, filled with bright colors, posters of superheroes, and the comforting clutter of a life yet untouched by the darker realities of the world.

Tommy's mother, Mrs. Phillips, was in the kitchen, humming softly as she prepared dinner. The scent of baking bread filled the house, mixing with the faint smell of cinnamon from a pie cooling on the counter. It was a typical evening in their household, a picture of domestic tranquility that had become all the more precious in the aftermath of the storm.

But Tommy's attention wasn't on his toys or the comforting sounds of his mother in the kitchen. He was focused on something else, something that had caught his attention moments before—a sound that didn't belong, a sound that had made the hairs on the back of his neck stand on end.

He had been playing with his action figures, staging an epic battle between the heroes and the villains, when he heard it—a faint whisper, barely audible, coming from the direction of his closet. At first, he thought he had imagined it, that it was just the wind or the creak of the old house settling. But then he heard it again, a soft, insistent sound that sent a chill down his spine.

Tommy froze, his small hands tightening around the action figure in his grasp. He listened intently, his heart beginning to pound in his chest as the whisper grew louder, more distinct. It wasn't just a sound—it was words, spoken in a voice that was both familiar and strange, a voice that seemed to come from somewhere deep within the shadows.

"Tommy... come here..."

The whisper was so soft, so gentle, that it almost sounded like a lullaby. But there was something wrong with it, something that made Tommy's skin crawl, that made him want to run, to hide. He glanced toward the closet, the door slightly ajar, and felt a wave of fear wash over him.

"Tommy... I need you..."

The voice was clearer now, more insistent, and Tommy felt a cold sweat break out on his forehead. He wanted to call out for his mother, to run to her and tell her what he was hearing, but something held him back, something that made him stay rooted to the spot, his eyes locked on the darkness beyond the closet door.

"Tommy... don't be afraid..."

The whisper was almost soothing, a tone that seemed to promise safety, comfort. But Tommy wasn't fooled. He could feel the wrongness of it, the way it seemed to wrap around him, pulling him in, urging him to step closer, to open the door wider, to see what was waiting for him inside.

But Tommy didn't want to go near the closet. He didn't want to see what was inside, didn't want to know where the voice was coming from. All he wanted was for it to stop, for everything to go back to the way it was before, when his room was just his room, and the world was a safe place.

"Tommy... please..."

The voice was pleading now, desperate, and Tommy could feel his resolve weakening, his fear battling with a strange curiosity, a pull that he couldn't quite resist. He knew he shouldn't go near the closet, knew that whatever was inside wasn't something he wanted to see, but he couldn't help himself.

Slowly, hesitantly, he rose to his feet, his small body trembling with fear and uncertainty. He took a step toward the closet, his heart pounding in his ears, the sound of the whisper growing louder, more urgent.

"Tommy... I'm waiting..."

He was almost at the closet now, his hand reaching out to touch the door, to push it open, to reveal whatever was lurking inside. But just as his fingers brushed against the wood, he heard another sound—a sharp, insistent knock on his bedroom door.

"Tommy? Are you okay in there?"

It was his mother's voice, filled with concern, and the sound of it broke the spell that had held him in place. Tommy jerked back, his heart racing as he tore his gaze away from the closet and looked toward the door.

"Yeah, Mom, I'm okay," he called out, his voice trembling despite his efforts to sound calm.

The door creaked open, and Mrs. Phillips stepped inside, her brow furrowed with worry. "You sure? You look a little pale, honey."

Tommy forced a smile, trying to push down the fear that still gripped him. "I'm fine," he said, though his voice wavered. "Just... just playing."

Mrs. Phillips nodded, though she didn't look entirely convinced. She crossed the room and knelt beside him, her eyes searching his face. "You know you can tell me anything, right?" she said gently. "If something's bothering you..."

Tommy hesitated, his eyes flicking back toward the closet for just a moment before returning to his mother's face. He wanted to tell her, wanted to explain what he had heard, what he had felt, but something held him back. Maybe it was the fear that she wouldn't believe him, that she would brush it off as just his imagination. Or maybe it was something deeper, something that told him that this was a secret he needed to keep, at least for now.

"I'm okay, Mom," he said again, this time with more conviction. "Really."

Mrs. Phillips studied him for a moment longer, then nodded, though the concern in her eyes didn't fade. "Alright," she said softly. "But if you need me, I'm just downstairs, okay?"

Tommy nodded, watching as she stood up and headed for the door. "Okay."

She paused at the doorway, glancing back at him with a smile that didn't quite reach her eyes. "Dinner will be ready soon. Come down when you're ready."

With that, she left the room, closing the door behind her with a soft click. The silence that followed was almost deafening, the peaceful sounds of the neighborhood outside a stark contrast to the tension that still thrummed in Tommy's chest.

For a long moment, he stood there, staring at the closed door, his heart slowly beginning to calm. But then, almost against his will, his gaze was drawn back to the closet, the door still slightly ajar, the darkness inside seeming to pulse with a life of its own.

He took a step back, the fear returning, stronger this time. He didn't want to go near the closet again, didn't want to hear that voice, that whisper that had promised comfort but had felt so wrong. He wanted to leave the room, to go downstairs and be with his mother, where it was safe and warm and normal.

But even as he turned to go, he heard it again—the whisper, soft, insistent, curling around him like a cold hand on his shoulder.

"Tommy... don't leave me..."

He froze, his heart leaping into his throat. The voice was different now, filled with a sadness that tugged at his heart, that made him want to stay, to listen, to understand.

But Tommy knew better. He knew that the voice, whatever it was, wasn't something he should listen to, wasn't something he should trust. He had seen enough movies, read enough books, to know that voices from the closet never led to anything good.

And yet, as he stood there, torn between fear and curiosity, he couldn't help but wonder—what if the voice was real? What if it was someone who needed his help, someone who was trapped, alone, afraid?

The thought sent a shiver down his spine, and he bit his lip, his hand twitching at his side. He should leave. He should go downstairs, forget about the voice, forget about the closet, forget about everything that had happened in the past few minutes.

But he couldn't. The pull was too strong, the curiosity too overwhelming. He had to know, had to see what was inside, had to understand where the voice was coming from.

With trembling hands, he reached out once more, his fingers brushing against the closet door, pushing it open just a little bit wider.

"Tommy..."

The voice was clearer now, more distinct, and as the door swung open, he saw it—a shadow, faint but unmistakable, shifting in the darkness, a figure that seemed to flicker in and out of existence, like an old film reel playing on a loop.

Tommy's breath caught in his throat, his heart pounding in his chest. He wanted to scream, wanted to run, but he couldn't move, couldn't tear his eyes away from the figure in the closet.

"Tommy... please...

help me..."

The voice was pleading, desperate, and Tommy felt a pang of something—sympathy, maybe, or pity. The figure was small, childlike, its outline blurred and indistinct, as if it were made of smoke. But the voice... the voice sounded so real, so human, so...

"Who are you?" Tommy whispered, his voice shaking.

The figure shifted, the shadows around it deepening, and for a moment, he thought he saw a face—pale, gaunt, with hollow eyes that seemed to stare right through him.

"Tommy... don't leave me..."

The words sent a chill down his spine, and finally, the fear overwhelmed the curiosity, breaking the spell that had held him in place. With a choked gasp, he stumbled back, nearly tripping over his own feet as he scrambled away from the closet, his heart racing in his chest.

He reached the door, his hand fumbling for the knob, and with a desperate pull, he yanked it open, the hallway beyond a beacon of light and safety. He didn't look back as he fled the room, his footsteps echoing down the stairs, his breath coming in ragged gasps.

Tommy didn't stop until he reached the kitchen, where his mother was setting the table, her back to him. The sight of her, so normal, so comforting, brought tears to his eyes, and he ran to her, burying his face in her apron, his small body trembling with fear.

Mrs. Phillips turned in surprise, her hands stilling as she looked down at him, concern flashing in her eyes. "Tommy? What's wrong?"

He didn't answer, just clung to her, his heart still pounding in his chest, the memory of the voice, of the figure in the closet, etched into his mind.

Mrs. Phillips knelt down, wrapping her arms around him, holding him close. "It's okay, sweetheart," she murmured, her voice soothing. "It's okay. You're safe."

But Tommy didn't feel safe. Not anymore. Because he knew, deep down, that the voice, the figure in the closet, was something more than just a figment of his imagination. It was something real, something that had found him, that had reached out to him, and that would be waiting for him, the next time he was alone.

The memory of the storm, of the darkness that had swept through the town, was still fresh in his mind, and he couldn't shake the feeling that it wasn't truly over, that something had been left behind, something that was still out there, lurking in the shadows, waiting to be found.

Tommy's grip on his mother tightened, and she rubbed his back, trying to calm him, to reassure him. But the fear, the unease, lingered in the back of his mind, whispering to him, just like the voice in the closet.

"Tommy..."

He could still hear it, faint but persistent, like a distant echo that refused to fade away.

"Tommy..."

It was a voice he knew he would never forget, a voice that would haunt him, that would stay with him, even in the safety of his mother's arms.

And as he clung to her, his eyes squeezed shut, he couldn't help but wonder—what if the echoes were never truly gone? What if the darkness, the force, still had a hold on Whistler's Grove, just waiting for the right moment to return?

The thought sent a shiver down his spine, and he pressed closer to his mother, trying to push the fear away, trying to hold on to the light, the warmth, the safety.

But deep down, he knew. The echoes were still there, still lingering, still waiting.

And someday, they would return.